MATING MISSION

A BBW Paranormal Shifter Romance

ANGELA FOXXE

Copyright ©2015 by Angela Foxxe & SimplyShifters.com
All rights reserved.

About This Book

When curvy Claire begins dating the mysterious Roman she feels like she has met a man with the full package. He is handsome and has the money and charm to go with it.

Everything about him is perfect. Well, almost everything.

Little does she know, Roman is an Alpha Shifter on a very particular mission. He must find and mate with a fertile human female as soon as possible.

The exact reason for his mission is a mystery but does this mean he actually has no interest in Claire as a person? Is this really all about "the mission"?

But most of all, what might actually happen if the Alpha's mating mission is a success?

READ ON TO FIND OUT..

Get Yourself a FREE Bestselling Paranormal Romance Book!

Join the "**Simply Shifters**" Mailing list today and gain access to an exclusive **FREE** classic Paranormal Shifter Romance book by one of our bestselling authors along with many others more to come. You will also be kept up to date on the best book deals in the future on the hottest new Paranormal Romances. We are the HOME of Paranormal Romance after all!

* Get FREE Shifter Romance Books For Your Kindle & Other Cool giveaways

* Discover Exclusive Deals & Discounts Before Anyone Else!

* Be The FIRST To Know about Hot New Releases From Your Favorite Authors

Click The Link Below To Access Get All This Now!

SimplyShifters.com

CHAPTER ONE
CHAPTER TWO
CHAPTER THREE
CHAPTER FOUR
CHAPTER FIVE
CHAPTER SIX
CHAPTER SEVEN

CHAPTER ONE

It's hard not to feel bad for yourself when all you can do is think about how happy everyone else is and how happy you aren't. I look at them, holding their newborn baby girl and I can't help but feel the yearning for my own. Not that I'm not thrilled for them, after all, they now have a beautiful, darling girl that they've wanted for so long. I just feel like I should be the one enjoying this slice of life. All I am is sitting here, or running around in circles, while the rest of the world is moving on. I feel like I've been forgotten.

"Wow, she's gorgeous," Desire says with a smile, looking into the room with me. I smile too, looking at the pink balloon and pink teddy bear that she's brought to the hospital for the baby. I brought my own bag of goodies for Chloe. I've been in this situation before and I know that a woman who has just been through giving birth wants nothing more than something to relax with, like a snack and a drink. I hate that I know all of this without actually experiencing it.

Truthfully, I've been one of those girls that most men find annoying or off putting. Yes, I've wanted children since it first struck me that the miracle of life was actually a genuine miracle. When I held my cousin Josey's baby in my arms, I was done for. It haunts me. Some people lay awake at night thinking about what they're going to do in life, but for me, it's always been babies.

Whenever I see them, I just melt at the sight of them. I want to have one to take care of and raise. But it takes two to tango, and I'm not ready to be a single mom. No, I want a man like Mark who will stand by me while giving birth, and will dote over our newborn with me. Chloe is so lucky to have Mark.

"I don't know what to do right now," Desire says, awkwardly standing in the doorway, watching the proud new parents glowing with excitement over their daughter. "Do we interrupt them? What do we usually do?"

"It depends on the parents, really," I tell her with a smile on my lips. "They seem pretty wrapped up in her. They'll probably be a while."

"Look how tiny she is." Desire shakes her head, a bewildered smile spreading across her lips. "Did they ever actually settle on a name or are they still bickering over that?"

"I don't know." I shrug again. "I got here like five seconds before you did."

"You must be so proud," Desire says after a moment. To be honest, I am. How can I not be? After all, I look in there and I see a baby that is half mine and half theirs. Chloe's eggs were next to useless and they needed a host egg. When they asked me, I thought it was the happiest day of my life. After all, looking in there, I'm seeing a glimpse at my future. One day, that will be my man in there, with me on the bed, holding our little baby. That will be the best day of my life. I have no doubt about it. As I take a deep breath, trying to hold back the tears, I nod to Desire. "Jesus, Claire, don't get so emotional about it," she says, laughing at me.

I laugh with her. I've always been a little crazy around babies, but that's not my fault. I'm just wired that way. Other people get crazy around sports or food. I get crazy around babies. After all, what's more incredible than having a sensuous night of passionate, fiery sex and conceiving a life out of the most incredible orgasm every shared by two people and then developing that life into a baby that I will get to nurture and care for.

God, people think I'm a freak for that, but what could possibly be better? Nothing. I don't think there's a single thing better.

"How was the hotel?" I ask her. All three of us met at the same place. As their manager, I'm technically not supposed to fraternize with Chloe or Desire, or even Maria, but they're too fun. Everything about the four of us is centered around laughter. In fact, I can't think of one night in the past five years where I haven't spent time with at least one of them, if not all of them. It's sort of our tradition.

"Maria's got it covered," Desire says with a sideways grin, the kind of grin that I know will get me into trouble later. She has a way of keeping me on my toes at work and when we're not.

Of the four of us, Desire has always been the most dangerous one. "All this lovey dovey crap is making me nauseous. I came here to see a baby, not the two of them making baby noises."

"Get used to it," I tell her with a grin of my own. "Chloe's officially a mommy."

"And already she's annoying." Desire shakes her head in revulsion. I know that she's kidding but it gets to me. She knows how badly I wanted to be the first to have a baby.

"It's adorable," I snap at her.

"Hey, that reminds me..." Desire grabs my arm and pulls me away from the doorway. Several nurses give us frumpy looks as they go about their business, ignoring us like we're stricken with the plague. "I saw Jake the other day."

"How does saying 'it's adorable' remind you of that?" I ask her. "And who cares?"

I do. Everything in my body screams out at his name, clawing and scrambling to try and get a hold of that name. I love Jake and he loved me, once upon a time. Five years of dating gone. I met Jake the first week I was working at the hotel. He'd come in as a guest, looking to stay somewhere nice and classy, a way for him show off his trust fund benefits.

Looking back on it, I always made fun of him for how arrogant and boastful he'd been in that first encounter.

But after five years, you think that you just might be able to change someone, even if you know it's a long shot. Maybe that's something other women do, or maybe it's just something specific to me, but I'm done trying to change men.

They're animals and that's all I need to know. Jake wanted to sleep with other women and I wanted him loyal. He got his other women and I was left with a broken heart. It's history, everyone's common thread, heartbreak. I'm not special, we all have it.

"I thought you might care since you used to bone him," Desire grunts with a shrug. "Or he used to bone you. I'm not sure what he was into."

"We're in a maternity ward, Dez,"

I shake my head at her crassness. There are some things that should be sacred around vulgar beasts like Desire. She just rolls her eyes and shrugs at me. After all, I know that she's just looking out for me. It's what friends do for each other.

They keep tabs on their exes, like monitoring a minefield for a fellow brother-in-arms. But seriously, after three months, the last thing I want to hear about is Jake.

"Did he look good?" I ask her somberly.

"Oh, God no," Desire shakes her head and scoffs. "He's homeless now and has herpes. He's a total nightmare."

I know that she's lying and it means a lot to me that she would try to protect me like that. I smile at her and touch her gently on the shoulder. "Thanks, Dez," I say, leading her back to Chloe and Mark. It's time to break up this love fest and get a little excitement going on in there.

"Have you lost weight?" Desire exclaims right through the doorway and I grin at my first glimpse of their tiny little miracle. She's wrinkly and pink and absolutely perfect in every possible way. Her eyes are closed and she eagerly drinks a tiny bottle that Chloe has been given by the nursing staff.

I take in every little detail about her, how she looks pale purple in some spots, like her hands and feet, and how rich and deep her pink is on her chest. I love the look of her. I love everything about her. It's strange to think that I donated an egg, half of her. Chloe looks at me taking in her daughter while Desire jokes with Mark.

"What do you think?" she asks me sweetly.

"I think she's perfect," I say through tears in my eyes.

"Yeah? I think so too," Chloe says with a great, pride-filled grin on her face. "Claire, thank you so much for this."

"Don't mention it," I say, kissing her on the forehead. We were with them as they looked at the costs of adoption and the unreal waiting period to get a child. It was overwhelming for them. When they got the costs and the procedure of using a host egg, it seemed like it was the only real option for them. They didn't want to wait years and years to start a family that they wanted now.

They were terrified of what might happen over that length of time. I was more than happy to offer my services. Wiping the tears away, I offer her the goodie bag that I made for her.

"So did you settle on a name?" I ask them, eager to hear what it was that finally stuck. Last I heard there were nearly twenty contenders.

"Katrina," Chloe says warmly and affectionately, staring deeply into the face of her new daughter. I smile at the name. I like it. It has an excellent ring to it.

After a while, I feel the welcome wearing down. Chloe is yawning heavily, trying to get control of her body, but losing the battle. She's just been through a major, physical trauma and we've been here taking up all their time.

"I should get going," I tell them finally. "I have to cover Matt's shift at the hotel."

"Boo," Chloe says, trying to pretend her hardest that she doesn't want me to go. I give her points for trying, but it's clear that she's exhausted. I don't hold it against her. I would be too. Anyone would want a moment just to rest for a second while their precious bundle of joy sleeps as well.

Wrapping my arms around her, I hold her tight, giving her a kiss on the cheek before hugging Mark tightly as well. "Thanks for this," he says in my ear. I nod to him before taking my purse and waving goodbye to them. Desire is picking at the cheese and fruit tray the nurses left for Chloe and Mark, offering me a slight nod. Clearly, she's not planning on picking up and leaving just yet.

Leaving the hospital, I take the chance to see as many babies as I can, passing the nursery window, looking at all the poor babies, alone in the world, wondering where their mothers are. I want to pick up each of them and hug them tightly, but I know that I can't. Instead, I gently place my fingertips on the glass, looking in at them with a smile on my face, sad and somber.

Walking across the parking lot, I make my way to my crimson Sentra, trying to stave off the hunger of wanting a child. In fact, all I can do is think about babies now.

On a regular day, I'll think about them whenever I see them, but today has been especially difficult. I'm sure that it'll take me a good week or so to get over little Katrina. But I'm okay with that. She's precious and I'm excited to watch her grow up.

Unlocking the door, I drop down in the driver's seat, feeling the pull of exhaustion and it's not even time for my shift to start. I still have an hour or so until I need to head to the hotel. I suppose that there's time for me to go grab a coffee or something before I head in. I sigh, I hate going to coffee shops. Even dressed as I am now, it's like throwing bloody chum into shark infested waters.

No one really cares about the plight of the more attractive women in the world and getting hit on. Most people think that it's a good problem to have, but honestly, I find it annoying. I don't work out and take care of myself because I want to lure men in. I do it because I like the way I look and I like the way it makes me feel.

That doesn't make me a slut or a tease, it just means that I like looking good. But most men think that it's because I want attention and all the wrong men are more than willing to give it to me.

So going to a coffee shop is never just a relaxing time to spend reading a magazine or the newspaper. Even if I have headphones in, they come up to me and wave their hands at me, asking if I'd like some company or wondering what I'm reading. It's annoying.

Starting the engine, I figure that I don't have much of a choice. I'm going to need to do something and if I head home, I'll just spend the whole time in traffic only to have five minutes before turning around and heading back in. As far as I'm concerned, it's a lose, lose scenario.

I take a deep breath and decide that it's the only logical thing to do, and head for the Starbucks near the hotel. There are half a dozen bakeries and small, privately owned coffee shops around the hotel, adding to its charm that allures so many of our customers. I try to avoid those. That's where people gather to hang out and lurk for attractive tourists. At Starbucks, everyone is in and out, efficiently. I like that. It keeps traffic moving, washing over me like a river.

It takes only twenty minutes to get to the Starbucks, thanks to freakishly light traffic. I groan as I pull into the parking spot and look at the coffee shop, wary of what's waiting inside. When I get out of the car, I try to rummage through my purse as I walk, praying that I have my iPod with me. Groaning at a failed attempt to find it, I pull open the doors, feeling the coolness of the air conditioning wash over me.

There's a dull roar that's a mixture of cool crooner music and soft conversations overlapping all around the busy coffee shop. I look at the short line in front of the register and take my place behind a man wearing a charcoal gray suit with a deep purple shirt.

With nothing else to do, I look at the back of his head. His dark hair is trimmed, softly spiked in a casual yet styled manner that is quite impressive to me. There's nothing quite like a man with style. The real trick, though, is to see if he's wearing good dress shoes. From his build, he clearly works out, but not too much. He doesn't overdo it. He has a nice ass that much is for sure. I look down farther expecting to see a loafer, or worse, tennis shoes. Instead, I notice that he's wearing a very nice, very clean pair of black leather shoes that remind me of Prince Charming, for some reason. Maybe it's the style or the silver bar on top, I can't really place it.

Unfortunately, when I look up, I notice that he's glancing over his shoulder at me. I know that he's caught me checking him out; I just hope he didn't catch me checking out his ass. God, it's so embarrassing when this happens. He offers me a crooked smile and I smile back. What am I doing? Don't smile back at a stranger! That's just inviting them to park it next to me and ask me inane, stupid questions while I whittle away the minutes, praying that I had a time machine.

I take in his features with my ill-conceived smile, noticing his strong jaw, his perfect cheekbone size, and the nice field of black stubble across his cheeks and chin, but absent from his neck, a good sign again.

For a moment, I feel confident that this stylish man is gay and that I'm safe, but deep down inside, I almost hope that he isn't.

"I got them half off," he says to me in a strong, rugged voice. I smile at the words coming out of his mouth, but I don't have the slightest idea what he's talking about. His eyes meet mine, piercing sapphires staring into my soul. His eyes glance down and I follow them, noticing that he's talking about the shoes. "They were a great deal."

"Oh," I say, feeling completely stupid. "That's always a great thing to find."

"So are friendly people," he says, unfolding his arms and stretching out his hand for mine. "Roman," he says with a crooked sort of grin that spells out trouble, usually. I shake my head, not believing that I'm actually going to do this. I shake his hand and feel how warm and strong his grip is.

"Claire," I say to him.

"Claire," he repeats with a contemplative tone. "I like that, it's old, aged with beauty. Haven't heard it for a while."

I can think of three Claires right now that I know of. But we run in different circles, I'm sure. I would have noticed a dashing man named Roman running around. I don't know what it is about him, but there's definitely a little magnetism. I think about Desire and how she lied to me about Jake looking terrible. I know that he's moved on, and yet, I'm still here, wallowing. I decide that three months has been long enough. I can have some fun once in a while too.

"You look like you're on your break," Roman says to me.

"No," I assure him, gaining my senses back. "Heading that way, though."

"Then you should go first," Roman says, stepping aside. "In fact," he turns to the woman behind the register who is smiling at us like a mannequin, "whatever she's having, I'm buying, just make it first. She's got places to go and important people to see."

"Oh, no," I shake my head, smiling. "You don't have to do that."

"No, please." Roman hands the woman behind the counter his debit card. "I insist. My treat."

"Thank you," I say, stepping forward to order.

*

The Chateau is a hotel that's designed to give an elegant, imperialist French accent to the world. When people step inside of the Chateau, they immediately have thoughts of Marie Antoinette, counts, and elegance conjured within their minds as they step through those front doors.

It's an opulent dream of an eccentric lottery winner from thirty years ago. In that time, he crafted and molded the perfect hotel in his mind and gave it a quaint, independence that very few hotels ever get the chance to see. With plenty of money to pour into the project, Jean made the Chateau into a wonder. Every week, conventions take place, groups stay for reunions, and celebrities sneak in under false identities.

I love the Chateau. It's the reason I've stayed with her for so long. She pays me well and I tend to her every need. As much as Jean loved this place before he died, I feel as though I love it more. As far as hotels go, it's magical and completely wondrous.

Stepping through the front door after Bernie opens it for me, delightful and chatty as ever, I look at the bellhops and attendants all scurrying around to their various duties. The restaurant and bar are in full swing and it looks like today is the start of another heavy week. I smile at the sight of it. I love this place so much. I lift my Pumpkin Spice Latte to my lips and take another drink, trying to shake off the lingering thoughts of Roman. It's time to work and fall traffic is picking up for us.

"Afternoon, Claire," Gina says to me as she rushes to the restaurant.

"Hi," I smile at her, making my way to my office. I'm going to be so pissed if Henry has junked the place again. I spend the first half of my shift cleaning up after that animal and I'm tired of it. He doesn't even need the office. Sarah does all the bookkeeping and I tend to all of the management and scheduling.

All Henry has to do is make sure that the place doesn't burn down when I'm not here. It's not that hard of a task. In fact, I'm pretty sure that a well-trained ape could replace Henry.

"Maria, how are you?" I ask, smiling at pretty Maria behind the counter. She looks up at me and smiles a bright, beaming grin. I'm pretty sure that they chased her out of Columbia for being too beautiful.

"How are things going?" I ask her, tossing my jacket onto a chair with my scarf.

"Who cares?" Maria cries. "Tell me all about her."

"Oh my God, Maria," I smile, thinking about little Katrina all bundled up.

"She's so wonderful, so precious. I just want to pick her up and squeeze her." I say with a huge dorky grin spreading across my lips as I mimic hugging a baby.

"I'm going to go see them first thing," Maria tells me excitedly. "I wish I could have been there."

"Me, too," I tell her, glancing into the office. Henry is devouring something that has come out of a grease-laden bag and I'm too afraid to find out what it is. I shudder at the thought of it. That man is an animal and I'm not afraid to tell anyone what I think about him. Why the powers that be decided to hire him is beyond me.

"So, what did he get done today?" I ask Maria.

"He dealt with a few angry customers in his own special way," Maria says out of the corner of her mouth, but while she's talking, I immediately block her out. It's not because I'm mean or can't stand listening to her, but because I stare with disbelief as Bernie holds the door open for Roman.

I watch him entering the hotel, reading a folded newspaper as he walks, with his Starbucks in his other hand, completely tuning out the world around him. I watch how he walks, perfectly. With such posture and pose that it's almost as if he has a soft, natural strut to the rhythm he walks to.

"Oh my God," Maria says, snapping her fingers. "You're totally tuning me out to check out Mr. Handsome over there, aren't you?"

"Sorry." I snap out of my daze. "I'm so sorry, Maria."

"No, I don't blame you," she says with a sly smile on her lips. "He's a handsome devil."

"What's he doing here?" I ask her.

"How should I know?" She laughs. "I think he's heading for the restaurant. Maybe he's meeting someone for business or something."

"Maybe a girlfriend." I feel my heart quivering.

"No way." She shakes her head. "You don't take a Starbucks and a newspaper to a date."

"Good eye." I nod, buying into that theory. I watch Gina smile at him and take him to the table he's seeking, As he vanishes, I can't help but feel terrified. I look at Maria who is inspecting every little thing that's happening right now with a scrutinizing gaze. "Stop looking at me like that," I tell her.

"Spill it," she says resolutely, ignoring the fact that I'm her boss.

"There's nothing to spill," I tell her sheepishly. "I was at Starbucks and he was in front of me and offered to buy my drink for me."

"What?" Maria grins excitedly. "Oh my God, Claire. Did you flirt with that man?"

"I did." I smile proudly.

"Good for you," Maria hugs me eagerly. "It's time for you to get out there and share Claire with the rest of the world. You know what I mean?"

"I do," I say to her with my chin held high. Turning, I grab my coat and scarf and feel brave enough to chase Henry the slob out of my office. "Hank, clock out," I tell him sternly.

As the hours pass, I keep working, watching as the shift changes and overseeing the smooth transition. Saying goodbye to Maria is hard because that leaves me with Rose and Margot who don't really care about anyone but each other.

They're the kind of best friends that come as a duo, never by themselves. It makes it hard for them to meld with others, so I try to keep them scheduled together. After all, they do good work together. So as long as it's not a problem, I don't see a reason to split them up.

Standing at the station tucked away by the wall, I listen to a woman on the phone telling me that I've messed up their arrangements and that I need to fix it immediately. I never mess up arrangements and I saved these dates for her myself.

We initial all entries to ensure that we have clear communication at the Chateau, so I know that I didn't mess up her booking. I keep the phone cradled between my ear and shoulder, listening to her talk to me about how it's very important to have good customer service.

It's almost laughable that I'm being subjected to this woman's lecture. She clearly has no clue who I am. I roll my eyes and keep listening to her, even though I changed her scheduled dates ten minutes ago.

When I look up, I feel a petrifying fear wrapping around my heart and lungs instantly, like I've been flash frozen. I stare up at the man standing on the other side of the counter, grinning at me. Without thinking, I lift up my index finger in a symbol to tell him to wait one moment. I suddenly feel that it was an incredibly rude gesture, but I don't have much to work with right now. He's caught me completely off guard and I feel like a complete moron.

"Well, it looks like the situation has been resolved," I interrupt the woman on the phone finally, tired of playing her game. The woman squawks at me as I slowly grunt at her that I understand and then hang up on her, rather suddenly.

I pray that the powers that be don't get a complaint from her. Actually, if she complains, it'll be me who gets it, so I'm inclined not to really care about it. Taking a deep breath, I look up at the man standing in front of me and offer him a friendly, professional smile.

"Roman from Starbucks," I say as pleasantly as I can muster while feeling like I'm an elementary school girl trying to throw a kickball at his head.

"I'm Roman from Starbucks?" he asks with a huge grin on his handsome face. "Are there a whole lot of Romans running around in your life?"

"When I'm in Rome," I say, trying to make a joke but instantly regretting it, hearing how incredibly stupid it sounds the moment it's verbalized. He graciously smiles at the terrible joke and gives me a moment of freedom from my shame.

Looking at him, I can't help but feel like he's here for something besides me. He couldn't possibly be here for me. I mean, he's too perfect, too handsome to be here for me. I have that stigma hanging on me like spider webs, that I've just gotten out of a serious relationship and that I'm not quite ready to take that final step into singledom.

"Is there something you needed?" I ask him, making sure that he's here for me and not to check into a room.

"No." He smiles at me. "I just came over to say hello."

"Are you stalking me?" I tease him for a moment, pretending that I didn't know he was in the next room the entire time. He laughs at that joke, smiling with a mouth full of perfect teeth.

18

"No, I actually was having lunch with a client," he says, pointing over his shoulder with his thumb toward the restaurant. I nod to him, acting like a student sitting in a lecture that she's really into.

"When I was coming out, I spotted you and was wondering if I'm just lucky or if you're some sort of spy keeping tabs on me."

"Oh, you think I'm stalking you?" I smile.

"Tables have turned, Claire from Starbucks." Roman grins at me, encouraging me on.

"Well, you're in luck," I say to him, trying to be clever but knowing that isn't my forte, I'm on shaky ground. I take it carefully from here.

"My cover has been blown, so I'm off the case."

"Good, so that means you're free to grab a drink with me?" Roman says.

He says it. I mean, I actually heard that, not just a voice inside my head. I stare at his face for a moment, baffled and completely caught off guard by this. I mean, he bought me a drink at Starbucks, but apparently that's not the end of this. Clearly he wants more.

He's not just doing this out of pity or out of boredom. I mean, he wouldn't ask that if he wasn't interested. This isn't just like a chuckle and a punch on the shoulder kind of friendship. You don't ask buddies for a drink, right? Crap, sometimes. I don't know. I think he's interested. Play it cool, I keep telling myself. Just play it cool, Claire.

"I'm due for a break," I tell him. Feeling dangerously curious and dangerously intrigued by him. Maybe I'm being reckless, but just maybe this is what I'm needing.

I look at the smile on his face and I can't help but feel like he's actually into this. "I'll be waiting for you," he says to me with a smile before turning and taking off toward the restaurant again. "Is there anything I can order for you?" he asks me.

"Just a Coke," I tell him, knowing that it's definitely against policy to have a drink while on the clock. I take a deep breath and look to see if Rose or Margot saw me getting hit on. I look down the bank of computers and see that they're too busy on Twitter or something else. Thank God. I take a deep breath and get ready to head for the restaurant.

Logging off the computer, I take the chance to try and figure out what I'm going to say, but I just have no clue what this is all about. Am I about to go on a date? While at work? I feel like a fool.

"Rose, I'm going to take a break," I tell her. "I'll be in the restaurant if you need me."

"Okay, have fun," she says ominously.

I'm suddenly terrified and confused. Did she see Roman hitting on me? Does she know all about it? I decide that I'm safe as I slowly back away from Rose, heading for the restaurant. As my heart pounds, I feel my body taking over, stealing from my brain, the right to walk. I follow his trail nervously, wondering where he's going to be leading me. With each step, the anticipation builds until I have a grand cathedral of anxiety taking up residency inside of my chest. I'm not sure what I'm doing, but it feels right. I should have done this a long time ago. This has been a long time coming.

I smile at Gina and point to where I'm heading.

I can see him, seated at a table for two, checking his phone for emails or texts or however it is that Roman from Starbucks spends his time on his iPod. I approach him cautiously, feeling like I'm encountering a wild snake or alligator on a nature program. I have to be smart about this. I don't want him catching on to how nervous or weird I am. I just have to play it cool, like jazz.

He looks up and glances around, searching for a sign of me. The moment his eyes hit me, it feels like someone turned a spotlight on and is following my movements. The enormous, charming grin on his face and the look of delight in his eyes makes him seem like he's actually excited for this.

Clearly he has no idea who I am. I'm not worth getting excited for. I take the final steps toward him until I'm finally standing in front of him, smiling politely. I'm not sure if this is a date, but I feel like that's the sort of thing you do on dates. You smile politely and act interesting.

"Glad I could wrangle you away," Roman says as I take the seat across from him. "Have you worked here long?"

"Wow, you must own the place by now," he jokes.

"Pretty much." I nod. "Without me, this place would fall apart."

"I don't doubt it," Roman says, dancing the line of jokingly sarcastic and serious. I know that he's not sure if I'm being serious. That's fine. I'll take the mysterious ground as long as I can. "This is one of the best hotels in the city."

"In the top five, every year." I feel myself boasting.

"Impressive. Unfortunately, this is actually the first time that I've been in here. I was having lunch with a client, going over some design choices."

That's bait; I know that much is certain. I decide right there that I'm not going to eat out of Roman's hand. I'm going to try and be mysterious, disinterested for a while.

I pick up the perspiring glass of Coke sitting in front of me and take a sip out of the straw, glancing out the window at a lady walking by in a large hat. You don't see very many people in large hats these days. I know that the silence is killing Roman as he glances out the window too, fidgeting with his glass.

"What did you have?" I ask him finally, mercy killing the silence for him. He looks at me with genuine excitement in his eyes that the conversation has picked up once more.

"The salmon," he answers eagerly. "It was so incredible. What was that rice stuff with it? That was the most amazing rice I've ever had."

"It's farro," I tell him. It is delicious. Most people ask that question.

"Wow, I'm going to have to look that one up," he says with a grin stretching ear to ear. "Can I ask you something?"

"I guess."

"How long since you broke up with him?" he asks me bluntly. I look at him, unamused by this line of questioning. I'm not going down this rabbit hole with a guy I met earlier today at Starbucks. "I'm sorry, but you have the look of the woman who just put down something long term."

"What look?" I protest that sort of comment vehemently.

"Like a fly caught in a web," Roman says very perceptively. "Like you want to get out of it, but you can't escape it."

I look at him, completely unhappy with what has transpired here. Why does a handsome, charming man want to discuss my last relationship? Why can't he discuss the possibility of us having a relationship? My eyes dart to his left hand, no ring. Maybe he's engaged and some sort of life coach.

Maybe I've sunk that low that life coaches are going to start throwing themselves at me. God, maybe I should get a life coach.

"Because," he says, dragging me out of my sorrow, "I am very interested in taking you out on a date, but only if you're interested too."

I look at him, surprised that he just said that. How could he just say that?

There's no way that he just said what I thought he just said. I blink several times at him before responding, trying to decide how to shape my words, other than 'uh huh.' As if waiting for my muses to sing to me, I let the silence swirl, stagnate. Finally, I take a deep breath and nod.

"Sure," I say with a shrug. "I'm interested."

CHAPTER TWO

"Is he there yet?" Desire asks on the phone while I peek out the blinds, keeping watch for any sign of him. I feel like Jimmy Stewart right now in Rear Window, but I'm spying on every car that passes by and every person walking on the street. I'm analyzing every one of them to see if it's Roman. With each passing second, I'm more and more certain that this is all some sort of elaborate joke.

I don't know who would do this, or how, and especially not the why of it, but I'm certain that it's a practical joke. Someone is going to jump out of my closet any second and shout, "Ah ha! Got you, Claire!" Even though I've checked the closets twice.

"No," I say anxiously. Looking at myself in the mirror, I know that I'm not as attractive as other women, but I do pretty great. I hate sounding immodest, but I've worked hard on my appearance. Being born beautiful has immense perks in life, no matter what people say about beauty not being that important.

In a sweater dress and boots, with one shoulder free, I look cute, but not overly sexy. Everything I own other than this is short, to show off my legs. I love my legs and so do all the men I've dated. But I don't want to look desperate or too nice. I just don't want to scare him off. I really like him.

After all, I spent thirty minutes talking with him at the restaurant and would have stayed there longer if Rose hadn't screwed up filling in the schedule and overbooking next Friday. He's an easy man to talk to and he has a charming demeanor. He's so mysterious in absolutely every way. I love the way he laughs and the way he keeps the conversation alive, no matter what topic comes up. He's so smooth and well versed in practically every topic. But the fact that he looks like he just stepped out of an advertisement for cologne doesn't hurt either.

"Are you going to sleep with him?" Desire asks me blatantly.

I smile at that question. It's very Desire to ask that. I close my eyes and think about it for a moment. I haven't been with anyone in three months. The week after Jake ended everything in a nuclear cloud of devastation, I had a one night stand with a guy I met at a bar and it was the worst experience of my life. There's nothing exciting or dangerous about it. I just woke up gross and not able to stand it.

He'd been a handsome enough guy, but he was completely infatuated with me. He showed up at my gym trying to ask me out again and I had to tell him bluntly that it didn't mean anything. So that pretty much ended my prospects of just running out and sleeping with a guy. I'm not that kind of a girl.

"You hesitated." Desire calls me out.

"No," I say defensively. "I'm not going to sleep with him."

I look out the window and see him approaching and feel a stone of anxiety crashing through the inside of my body, shattering everything as it plummets to the depths of my stomach. I feel like I want to scream.

"I would," Desire says on the other end of the phone. "If he's as hot as you say he is, then I definitely would get better acquainted with him."

"He's here," I tell her.

"Shut up." Desire laughs. "Hang up the phone, stupid."

For once, I'm inclined to listen to Desire. I end the call and quickly stuff my phone into my purse, checking my hair one last time in the mirror. A cascade of wavy, golden hair running down over my left shoulder, something Jake used to love. It feels blasphemously delicious, letting another man appreciate it. When I hear the knock on my door, I try to steady my heart, calm myself to act normal. Grabbing my coat, I calmly open the door.

On the other side, Roman is waiting for me. He looks spectacular in another suit that looks like he definitely had it custom made for him, or at the very least tailored to fit his body perfectly. I admire him in it, a dark, inky black suit with a royal blue shirt on underneath with a vest over it.

He has the look of a man who could be anything or anyone. He could look dangerous, but not threatening. I like it. He's handsome and I'm grateful that the first man I'm dating since Jake isn't a troll. In fact, I'm extremely happy that he's a man that I could definitely see myself going all the way with him. Oh God, I just pray that he doesn't have an STD. You have to be careful with guys like Roman, the handsome, sexy player types. Why am I thinking about this?

"You look incredible," Roman says, the first words he's said to me since I opened the door and we both were finally given a chance to visually feast upon each other. I look at his handsome smile, his luminous eyes, and I feel myself smiling back at him, grateful and unashamed.

"Thank you," I say, totally flattered by his personality. "You look great too."

"Nothing compared to you," he says.

I hope he's being genuine, even if I know it's a lie. People are going to wonder who the homeless woman is with that handsome man, but I'm fine with it. I could definitely see myself taking ownership of Roman, calling him my Roman. I notice that once again, he's not wearing a tie. I like that about him. It's very casual and yet he pulls off a debonair air about him.

"You're not a fan of ties," I note to him.

"No, actually." He grins and looks at his chest. "I think they feel like collars."

"Don't want to be on a leash," I say, closing the door behind me and stepping out into the brisk, autumn night. "I get that."

"Oh I don't mind being leashed," Roman answers, stepping back and giving me some privacy with my door. I know that he's flirting with me, but I pretend not to notice. I don't want to play too easy for him.

"It's just being collared that doesn't work for me, like I'm some sort of dog."

I'm going to file that away in the databank of things wrong with Roman. He clearly has dog issues or commitment issues. I pray to God that it's dog issues.

When I turn around, I see that he's offering me his arm, something so antiquated that it takes me a moment to realize what he's doing. I smile at the gesture, feeling like I belong in a Jane Austen novel right now. Taking his arm, I walk uncomfortably close to him as we go down the steps.

He doesn't say anything for a moment, walking on the sidewalk past the trees that are abandoning their leaves for the rest of the year. I look over him, stealing a glance of his face from the side, admiring how perfect his nose is. It hasn't been broken. It's not crooked or turned up like a snout. I like it exactly how it is. Jake's nose had always had this turned up look that distracted me.

"I've never walked with someone like this," I confess to him finally.

"Really?" Roman says with an eyebrow lifted, like I've been hiding under a rock somewhere. "I usually hold off on this sort of behavior until later on in a relationship, but I have to admit that I like you, Claire, so I'm making an exception."

I smile at that. "I'm glad you'll make me an exception," I say to him.

"Only for the best," he says, gesturing to a black car parked by a tree. "This is me," he says finally, opening the door for me and holding it like a gentleman. I'm afraid that he's trying a little too hard, that he's not being completely genuine or trying too hard to win me over. I give him an appreciative smile before getting into the car. He shuts the door behind me and rushes around the front of the car to the driver's door and quickly gets in, starting up the car and flooding us with a soft concerto that I don't recognize.

"Okay, Claire, we've had coffee and drinks already, so by my count this is the third date, but also the first, catch my meaning?"

"Absolutely, I would be disappointed if you did the same thing twice."

"It would be dreadful," he agrees, pulling out into traffic. "I could just see the newspaper headlines tomorrow. The media would tear me apart and you would be scandalized for the rest of your life. It would be the most dreadful and horrible thing ever to happen. The very apocalypse would commence."

I grin at that. "I don't think that it would be that bad."

"You'd be wrong." He smiles. "So in order to avoid a scandal, we'll do something I hope you'll enjoy."

I look at him, worried about what is in store for me tonight. There's something incredibly and excitingly enigmatic for me. As I look forward, toward the street lined with lights, I watch eagerly to see where we're going. I glance over at Roman, stealing a look of him. It's risky, but I'm eager to see him. He's too focused on the road to notice me, but I do catch him stealing a glance at my legs. I smile at this. It's something that warms me inside.

For a while, we drive in silence before he finally starts to talk about where we're going. He doesn't ask me a million questions to hastily get to know me or to pull the date in a direction I'll enjoy more. Instead, he just tells me about where we're going, how it's antiquated, a symbol of a bygone time. It's a bistro and dance club that's designed in the style of the Roaring Twenties. I smile at the sound of that. It sounds exciting, alluring even. With that in mind, I eagerly watch where we're going, enjoying every second of his explanation. I remain silent for most of the time, but he keeps the conversation alive for the both of us.

When we finally arrive, he parks the car on the side of the street and rushes around the car to open the door for me. I step out of the car and look at the club. It's classy, fancy even, but not overly gaudy. Roman offers me his arm and takes me toward the club.

The man at the door, waiting for visitors, nods to Roman and opens the door for us. Inside, it's exactly what I would envision in a dream built upon the foundation of the Great Gatsby. I look around with a grin on my face. The big band up on the stage plays and I feel the drum in my heart.

"What do you think?" he asks me with a grin on his face as well.

"This place is amazing," I tell him.

"It's kept pretty quiet actually," he says. "More people should stop by. It's a blast."

We're escorted to a table by a flapper girl who looks over Roman before handing us the menus for the night. I feel a sting of jealousy as I look at the woman walking away.

Talking about the items on the menu, we each settle on our desired meals. I order a dirty martini, watching Roman as he drinks his whiskey neat, not something I'm used to seeing. Jake was a beer man, but Roman quickly admonishes that he's never had a beer, nor will he ever. He's all about hard liquor apparently. I find that slightly sexy, so long as he's not a drunk. From what I can tell, he's not.

"What do you like to do, Claire?" Roman asks me as his steak arrives and my salmon is set before me. It smells like succulent butter and savory dill, filling my nose and making my stomach grumble eagerly.

"Other than go to Starbucks and run an entire hotel?"

I smile, trying to get a handle on what I want to tell him. My life isn't overly interesting or mysterious. In fact, my life is extremely dull without my friends around. From what I've experienced, men like girls who are exciting, beautiful, and dumb. I only have one of those features and it's usually just the gateway to the others.

People aren't looking for intelligent, alluring women. No, that's power and that scares them. What they want are dumb and pretty. When they find out that I have a brain inside of my head, they get scared.

"I don't do much," I tell him honestly, deciding to get this over quickly. If anything, I'll be able to have a new location to take my friends to. If there's anything that I've come to know clearly it is that men get tired of me. "I've put my career first."

"So have I," Roman confesses too. "But I have certain family obligations that keep me fairly leashed. Do you have family?"

I shake my head. "My mother died in a car wreck when I was a teenager," I tell him bluntly, like rubbing my fingers over an old scar. "My father is a drunk somewhere up in Alaska. I don't keep in touch with him very often."

"I understand the hardship of family," Roman says in a dour voice. "There are a lot of people out there that take their mundane families for granted. What I'd give to have a normal, boring all American family."

I smile at that. He's sweet. I'm glad he doesn't sugar coat it or try to console me on something that I've gotten used to. I look out on the dance floor. There are only a few people out there, but I'm jealous of them. I haven't been out dancing for a few weeks now. Since Chloe's pregnancy, it's been hard to get Desire and Maria to go dancing with me. Maria is great and always up for dancing, Paulo, her newest beau isn't, though.

"So tell me about him," Roman says, drawing my gaze from the dance floor. I look at him as he glances out at the others on the dance floor for a moment and clears his throat.

"About who?" I play ignorant. I'm not interested in delving into the past right now.

"The guy," he says, pushing deeper and deeper. "I think as the prospective new boyfriend, I have a right to know which particular minefields to avoid. I find it easier to avoid shit than stepping in it blindly."

I smile at that. Fair point. "He broke up with me after I found out that he was cheating on me," I tell him. "After I confronted him, he swore he could change and that it was an accident. After a few days of tears and desperate romantic gestures, I consented to give him a second chance."

Roman winces at that. "Never a smart move," he interrupts, seeing exactly where this is going. If he only knew the half of it.

"A week later, he broke up with me," I conclude a long story

abruptly.

"Asshole," Roman says with a bewildered and perplexed look on his face. Lifting his whiskey, he holds it up as if to toast. Begrudgingly and aching from the topic, I lift my martini up to meet his.

"His loss is my gain, and I do mean loss. He's going to be kicking himself forever, Claire. I guarantee that. You're going to haunt that man for the rest of his miserable life."

I clink my glass against his, but clearly I'm not sold on that idea. Desire, Chloe, and Maria have all given me the same pep talk, but I don't think Jake spends a second thinking about me. Taking a drink from his toast, Roman dabs his lips with his napkin and stands up, extending his hand to me. "Come on," he says bravely taking in a deep breath. "I owe you a dance after that. It was brutal."

"Oh no." I shake my head. "You don't have to."

"I insist," he says with a charming smile on his lips. I look at his handsome face and I can't help but feel like I'm the luckiest girl in the world. I don't know though. I haven't danced with a man since Jake and it's all a bit sudden feeling. I'm not good with just jumping in and doing crazy and exciting things. "Claire," Roman says finally. "Will you dance with me?"

I look at him, feeling bravery fighting through the doubt, like an explorer slashing through a tangled forest of anxiety and restrictions, fighting for the surface, fighting for the sunlight. I look up at him and feel the pounding in my heart building more and more. When I look into his dark sapphire eyes, I can't help but feel like I'm lost, adrift at sea, searching for land. I reach out, taking his hand. When our fingers touch, I could swear that he feels like dry land.

*

Call it a romantic indiscretion. Call it stupid, slutty, or completely insane, but the moment the door flings open, I wrap my fingers around his jaw, his perfect cheekbones, and I pull him close, wrapping my lips over his and feeling the passion ripping through us like a lightning bolt piercing a sacred oak, creating a miracle and giving life where only doubt and darkness once lurked.

I feel his hands on my waist and they beckon to me, pulling me closer as I breathe in, filling my nose with the scent of his cologne and feeling completely submerged into the depths of Roman. He pulls me closer, sliding his hands up my sides, gripping my ribs, sliding around to my back, embracing me and pulling me closer.

"I don't usually do this," I gasp, pulling away from him for a second. "Actually, I've only done it once."

"What? Sex?" Roman lifts an eyebrow.

Wow, he's clearly thinking he's in for more than he actually is. I don't think I would be bold enough to assume that a classy woman I was out on a date with would be slutty enough to put out, but clearly, I've given off that image and I'm going to have to live with that, because right now, I want Roman. I want him inside of me and I want him right now.

"No, sleep with a guy I just met," I tell him, stepping back into the darkness of my hallway, while he closes the door. Normally, I would be terrified that he might have a knife or a gun hidden on him, but after the club, there's nothing on him that I haven't already felt.

Sure, there was the dancing at first, then the close dancing, and then the extremely close dancing. Then there was the kissing at the table, then the kissing outside, then the making out in the car before I relented and told him to get back to my apartment as quickly as possible.

"Everyone starts out as strangers," Roman says, slipping off his suit jacket and tossing it onto the writing desk near the door. The way he does it is so effortless and smooth that it's infuriating. Only guys on TV shows and in the movies can do that. "This is the natural order of things. It's all part of civilized society. We're not animals after all."

"Sometimes we are," I say to him, chewing on my lip. I feel completely entranced by him and I've only had two drinks. I'm not a lightweight either. I've had my fair share of drinking contests and late night wine chats with my friends.

I watch Roman following after me, taking out his cufflinks as he walks, grinning eagerly as he approaches me, like a wolf closing in on his prey. He rushes at me and grabs me. I let out an excited squeal when his hands grip my sides and he pushes me gently against the wall, placing his lips on mine and kissing me passionately.

It's a kiss that feels like it's strong enough to cause sparks to start jumping from our lips. I feel him against me and all I can think to do is give in to him. I want him. I want this so badly. I don't know what that says about me as a person and I don't think I care, either. All I know is that I have deprived myself for too long. It's time for me to have some fun.

His hands are gentlemen, just like he is and just like he isn't. They feel my body, blindly exploring the musculature of my abdomen, seeking and absorbing all there is to appreciate. I let his fingers feel my abs, my sides, and my ribs. They're polite, easing me into what's to come.

My hands, on the other hand, are complete dogs. My fingers work blindly, unbuttoning his shirt and sliding it off his shoulders the moment I have it free, letting it drop to the ground. All the while, he kisses me, keeping me against the wall as he pulls away, looking deeply into my eyes.

I close my eyes, tilting my head back and letting him kiss me. Letting him have me. His hands are getting bolder and bolder, reaching up and feeling my breasts, gently cupping them over my bra. I smile at the feeling, the sensation of desire flooding through his touch. He kisses my cheek, and works his way down my neck as I feel the tingling, the static excitement of lust erupting all over me as he makes his way to my shoulder. I dig my fingers into his back and guide him to the bedroom.

Pushing open the doors, I feel him driving me back until I'm at the bed when he gives me a push. I feel like I'm floating for a fleeting second, drifting through the air until I land on my bed and within a heartbeat, Roman is right on top of me, kissing my neck and looming over me. I smile at the feeling and gently run my hands up his sides, feeling his toned and tight body underneath.

"Gym rat," I accuse him with a smile on my lips.

"Look who's talking." He looks up at me with a smile on his lips. It's the kind of look that makes me warm inside, that makes me want him even more. Feeling his body, I slowly slip my hands down, feeling how hard he is through his pants and not being disappointed in the slightest. I feel how long his is, how hard he is, and I'm more eager than ever to have him inside of me.

It's not small by any means and it's not too big like those hung guys that feel like they're entitled to ram it into you. I smile as I can feel his hips working, grinding his cock against my hand. I give him a squeeze and feel the shudder rippling through him. I love it. I love the effect it has on him.

As I work my way back up to his belt buckle, loosening it and beginning to slip it out of his loopholes, his phone begins to ring. It startles me enough that I freeze in the middle of what I'm doing. I look up at his face as he melts into a grimacing mask of disappointment. Shaking his head, we listen to the sounds of violins filling my bedroom.

"It's my family," he says with exhaustion poisoning the words in his mouth. He hangs his head, almost as if he's defeated by the sound of the ring tone. Slumping over to the side, I look at him, confused by all of this. Is his family situation that important that he has to go right now? Right in the middle of all of this? Fishing the phone out of his pocket, he glares down at the tiny screen illuminating his face in a glow of pale blue light that softens his features, making him looking like some stygian shade.

"I'm sorry for this, Claire," he says, shutting off the phone and running his fingers through his hair.

"Oh, no, it's fine," I tell him, sitting up and fixing my dress. "Is everything okay?"

"Not really." Roman sighs heavily. He looks over at me and suddenly sits straight up, bolting up like there's a board on his back and it's been lifted up to a ninety degree angle. "Hey, I've got an idea," Roman says with a deviously excited look in his eye.

I feel a little nervous with that look. Already, after just one night, I feel like I know Roman better than I've known Jake. I feel like he's a man without secrets and sometimes that's a terrifying notion.

"Claire, what are you doing tomorrow? It's Friday, so you have to have some sort of plans scheduled?"

I blush at the obvious misconception about the excitement detailed in my life. I shake my head and offer him a smile, politely. "You don't have to do this," I say. "I know when a guy isn't interested."

"Is that what was going on just now?" Roman asks me with a mischievous smile on his lips.

"My family is a priority in my life that I cannot ignore. When they ring the bell, I come running, that's just how it works, for now. But that doesn't mean I can't work around it and have some fun on the side. So, rather than go to a party at my father's house tomorrow night alone, listening to a bunch of annoying trophy wives and stodgy businessmen, perhaps you'll come along as my liaison to the real world."

"Liaison to the real world?" I lift an eyebrow, slightly intrigued.

"Yes, a prestigious title," Roman continues with his joke. I love that he takes things too far. "One that will be the envy of every woman and man in the world. Besides, I have some unfinished business with your body."

"Maybe this was your one shot," I say to him with a teasing shrug, holding my ground.

"Then damn my father for all eternity," Roman says as he stands up, buckling his belt. "But, that doesn't mean I won't try to win a second chance at winning another date with you for the rest of the night, regardless of where things end up."

His jovial smile melts away and a serious look covers his eyes and lips, softening the excitement that sharpens all of his features. "I like you, Claire. A lot."

I feel my heart flutter and a tremor racing through my body. That feeling is empowering, electrifying as I look at him, trying to hide my feelings from bursting out through my expressions. I look at Roman now in a new light, not just a fling or a quick run in the bed. I like the idea of him seeing more in me than just a casual sex partner or someone to flirt with and feel pity for.

Hearing that someone likes you is better than finding money on the ground, at least to me it is. I feel like a little girl who just got pecked on the cheek by the cutest boy in class. It makes me feel stupid, but completely smitten.

"I think I like you too," I say to him.

He smiles at that. "So do you have plans tomorrow night?" he asks me.

"I've got nothing," I say, shrugging at him. "Why, what's going on?"

"My father is throwing this big masquerade party," he says dismissively as if he's telling me about what happened in the stock market today. I look at him with a smile on my face as he talks.

"It's going to be big and fancy and completely boring, but at least I'll be there, which might be marginally appealing to you. But it would be extremely exciting if you're there with me. Oh, and there will be dancing, lots of dancing. For being as old as he is, my father does know how to throw a pretty enjoyable party if you drown out everyone else who is there."

"That sounds like a lot of fun." I smile at him.

"Excellent," he says with a big grin on his face, but it suddenly melts away like ice thrown into an oven. "Wait, that means you'll go with me, right?"

"Yes."

"Fantastic."

***

"You're joking," Desire says, pretending to be doing something at the computer. "Shut up. You're lying to me. Shut up, Claire. And you didn't sleep with him?"

"No," I tell her, angrily. I look at her and shake my head. She clearly thinks I'm a slut. "He had some sort of family emergency."

"So he just left? Like that? Right when you were getting to the good part?"

Desire lifts an eyebrow and shoots a glance at Maria. Maria grins mischievously, definitely in my corner.

Desire might be picking up red lights, but there's nothing unusual about that. After all, he alluded to the fact that his family comes first, something that doesn't really bother me. If something happened at the Chateau, I would be forced to leave while we were in the middle of something if I got the call. We all have our priorities, especially if we're in a new relationship.

"Well, do you know what you're going to wear?" she asks me.

God, I would love to spend the rest of the day shopping for the perfect dress, but there's no time for that. If he's picking me up tonight, I'm going to have to go with something I already own, which will be fine. All of my dresses are new to him right now. I thank God that I have that going for me and there are quite a few dresses that I've been looking for a reason to show off once more to the world. I think tonight will be my opportunity.

"You take your phone and call me if it gets weird," Desire says with a serious tone, like I'm dating a mass murderer. I nod at her. She's only weird because she cares so much. Looking down, I sign out of the computer and walk back toward the office, trying to figure out what tonight is going to be like.

"You like him?" Maria asks from the doorway, leaning on the frame. I look up at her and see the grin on her face. I can't help but smile at her.

"Yeah, I think he's pretty great," I say honestly. "Last night was a lot of fun, even before we started kissing. He just seems like a genuine guy, like there's no patience to hide anything. He is who he is, unapologetically. You know?"

"I knew a guy like that once." She nods. "He was an asshole."

"He totally could be, if he wanted to." I laugh at the idea of Maria having the patience for hanging around with an asshole. She probably ditched him halfway through the date. "But he's not. He's actually very sweet."

"Good." Maria nods. "But seriously, if this party blows, give us a call and we'll be there with baseball bats to knock some heads in and get you out of there. It'll be professional-like. We saw Zero Dark Thirty."

"They killed Bin Laden in that movie." I furrow my brow.

"I know what I said," she says in a stoic, cold voice. "No one messes with Claire and lives to tell about it." I watch her as she backs out of my doorway and I wonder what kind of a life Maria lived before coming to the United States.

Looking back at my own computer, I finish filling out statements and reports for the day, leaving messages for Henry when he comes on. I can't wait for Chloe to get back from maternity leave, but that'll be in like a billion years. Until then, I'm pretty much on my own with Henry.

Grabbing my coat, I close the office door behind me and look across the lobby to make sure that there's nothing immediate that demands my attention before I leave. Thankfully, all I see are a bunch of happy tourists going about their business or admiring the décor of the place. The sight of happy people makes me happy, especially when they're in my hotel.

"Do you have pepper spray?" Desire asks me as she scrolls through her Facebook feed on the computer.

"No." I shake my head.

"You should buy some." She shrugs. "Just in case."

"Don't listen to her," Maria says to me. "Have fun tonight."

"I will," I say, hugging her. "Take care of Henry tonight."

"When can I have his job?" Desire asks me as I hug her too.

"Soon," I say, almost considering it, for a moment at least. "Take care, you two."

As I cross the lobby, I glance over at the restaurant and catch a glimpse of a man who is looking right at me. He's holding a cell phone to his ear and the moment I lock eyes with him, his eyes narrow, as if he wasn't expecting to be seen.

His eyes are a pale blue, almost gray, the kind of eyes you'd attribute to wolves. They're freaky and alarming. He's wearing a T-shirt with a blazer over it, a strange sort of casual look. After a moment, he looks down at his hands, brushing crumbs off the table as he keeps talking to the person on the other end of the phone.

I don't know why it's unnerving to me, but I feel my feet hastening as I make my way through the revolving door. Bernie waves to me, mildly offended and surprised I didn't step through the door he was holding open for me.

"Sorry, Bernie," I call over my shoulder to him. "Have a good night."

"You too, Miss Claire," he shouts after me as I head for the parking lot.

With every step I take toward my car, the farther away I get from that man in the restaurant. Trying to shake off my uneasiness, I unlock my car and drop down into the driver's seat, quickly sticking the keys in the ignition.

I try to steer my mind back toward the date tonight. I don't think I've been to a masquerade since college and that one was fairly lame. I smile at the thought of something truly epic and spectacular. I hope it's a magical night like some sort of fairy tale dream. I know that I'm being silly and overly romantic about all of this, but it's nice to feel something other than bitterness deep inside of me. I back out of my parking spot and head for the street, turning and glancing at the entrance as I pull out.

The stranger is standing in the doorway, looking up and down the street with his phone still to his ear. There's something about him that's not right to me,
 that makes the hair on the back of my neck stand up. I pray that he doesn't see me as I head in the opposite direction, checking my rearview mirror and then see him walking the other way.

I'm imagining things. I'm just being silly.

CHAPTER THREE

I look at myself in the mirror, trying to decide if what I'm going for is something a little too fancy or if I should tone it down a little. After all, I have no clue what it is I'm getting myself into. I don't want to show up looking like I'm in way over my head, or look like I'm trying way too hard. Who knows? I've never been to something like this.

I've barely spent any time at a formal party, except on the rare occasion that Jake would take me to one of his father's or mother's events. Those happened around the holidays, but that was it. Usually, if I was lucky, we'd stay for half an hour and then we'd split. This will be the first time I've been to a formal party in a long, long time.

The woman who is looking back at me in the mirror is someone who looks great and I feel very proud of the figure that I've achieved. It's been a lot of work at the gym and this will be fun to actually have the chance to show it off a bit.

I hope my dress is not too similar to the one I wore last night. It's slinky, red and it's showing off one of my shoulders. This is easily one of the best dresses that I own and I'm eager to see what Roman thinks about it. I can't believe I care that much. I haven't cared about what anyone has had to say about me in months, not since Jake. Since Jake, I've been bitter and broken. It's nice to feel something new.

Picking bangles that match my dress perfectly, I slip them on my wrist and pick out my earrings. The woman standing in my mirror is complete, ready for whatever this night has to offer. I give myself a smile and turn toward the door, waiting for the knock, waiting with much anticipation.

When the knock finally does come, I feel as though my heart might burst out of my chest. Everything inside of me feels weak, eager to let this evening begin. As I draw closer and closer to the door, everything feels right, like the stars have aligned and everything is clear. I've never felt like there's something out there that resembles fate, but right now, I have the moment seized, captured in my hands, praying that I don't screw up tonight, that I don't ruin what I want so badly.

As I pull open the door, I look at Roman standing on the other side. He's wearing a deep purple suit, something that looks like he's out of a surreal movie. His black shirt and a tie that matches his suit makes the look powerful and exciting; it stuns me. He smiles at me, holding a white box in his hands with silver ribbon wrapped around it.

"You look ravishing," he breathes, as if he's exhaling in as much of a bewildered stun as I am. I love the sound of his voice fluttering like my heart is. It's so good to feel something that's reciprocal. Taking a deep breath, I smile at him, flattered by what I hear, what I'm feeling right now. I can't help but feel like I'm the luckiest woman in the world.

"You look pretty great yourself," I say with a twitterpated sigh.

He hands me the box in his hands with a grin on his face. "This is for you," he says.

Feeling the box in my hands, there's something electric about it. I love the feeling of it, the sensation of a gift is strange. There's a power in that feeling. I try to think of the last time I was given a real gift and not for my birthday, or Christmas, or even on Valentine's Day. A random gift is something special. I know that there's a possibility that he's trying to buy my affection, using his undeniable wealth to try and captivate me. The prospect of having someone try this desperately to garner my affection is quite flattering, if not a little mysterious.

"What is it?" I ask him, feeling the tickle of anticipation deep inside of me. I'm feeling incredibly excited about this. If he'll just tell me, it'll save the suspense.

"And ruin the surprise?" he asks me with a jovial smile on his lips.

Stepping back into my apartment, I set it down on the writing desk, looking over my shoulder at Roman who is cautiously, politely keeping his distance at the doorway. I like how appropriately gentlemanly he is. It's kind of like I'm dating Mr. Darcy after getting a bit of energy injected into him. "Can I open it now?" I ask him, feeling brave and bold all of the sudden.

He grins at me and leans against the door-frame. "Actually, I need you to," he says with a chuckle.

Finding that intriguing, I reach down and take the silver ribbon between my fingers and gently pull the bow apart. Letting it fall down on to my desk, I grab the lid of the box and gently lift it off, looking at the purple tissue paper inside, glittering and sparkling in the light of my hallway. Pulling it away, I look down at a beautiful white mask that looks like it's in the shape of a rabbit's head. I look down at it, the craftsmanship is flawless, handmade from the looks of it. There's a symmetrical pattern of diamonds speckled across the face of the rabbit, or at least they look like diamonds. The sight of it seems like something that belongs in a fancy photo shoot or on display somewhere elegant and lovely.

"It's beautiful," I breathe, gently taking the piece in my fingers as I lift it up, holding it to my face, looking in the mirror at my green eyes behind the mask. I look at the elegant mask on my face, matched with my dress and I feel something warm fluttering inside of me. "I'll give it back to you at the end of the night," I tell him, assuming that this is some sort of priceless heirloom or gift that his family is letting me borrow for the night.

"That's not how gifts work," he says with a grin.

"This is too much." I shake my head. "I can't accept this."

"After tonight, you may think that it's too little," he says with a strange sort of certainty in his voice. That makes me a little nervous. What am I getting myself into? Should I actually be worried about this? All this time, I just thought about the date aspect, being next to

Roman, mostly. I hadn't even thought about his family. The prospect of them being truly that terrible had pretty much escaped me. Everyone thinks their family is the worst, but what if his truly is?

I smile and hold the mask up to my face. For the first time, Roman crosses the threshold of my door and comes into the house. I watch with a smile on my lips as he takes the ribbon and ties it behind my head, gently working around my hair, careful not to mess anything I've worked so hard to achieve. I appreciate that. I'm grateful for that. As he ties it, I look at myself in the mirror, savoring the look of him behind me, the two of us together.

It's a sight that I would honestly like to see more of, because I want there to be an us. I find that funny. I've never thought about anyone like that before. Until this moment, I've always wondered who I'm going to end up with in the end of my hunt for a man, but not with Roman. I can actually see us. It's like looking into the future right now.

Of course, in the future, I won't be wearing a rabbit mask.

"How do I look?" I ask him.

"Incredible," he says with a smile on his lips. "Everyone's going to want to know who you are."

"Sounds like a lot to live up to," I say, feeling slightly uneasy about that.

This is technically our second date, no matter what he says, and I'm already meeting his parents. Not only am I meeting his parents, but I'm going to be completely submerging myself into his life and affairs. That's usually something that comes down the road months away. I take a deep breath. Apparently sometimes you have to jump into the deep end to get a chance to swim.

"You'll be great," he says, putting his hands on my arms.

* * *

There are more sparkling, glittering cars gathered in the enormous parking area of the mansion than I've ever seen before. I've been to a lot of car shows too. During college, I used to make money as a showgirl at car shows with my friends. It was an easy way to get money and it was an even easier way to get up close and personal with some of the hottest cars around. But everything I went to pales in comparison to this. In the dark veil of night, everything looks black and glimmering. It's beautiful, unlike anything I've seen before.

That of course, is nothing compared to the wrought iron fence that I came through with Roman. Elegant and ornate, the gate opened up, revealing the forested driveway that led up to the glowing mansion. It's the kind of mansion that you expect to see on the English countryside. I look up at the white walls, ornately decorated with columns, gargoyles, and statues.

There are fountains with stone figures, standing amidst the water, frozen in time with their perfect, flawless shapes and curves. The lawn is perfectly manicured, dotted with rich landscaping that's artistically laid out before the house, complimenting every feature, every aspect of the structure. It's something beautiful and lovely. I look at it all with hungry eyes, feeding on the beauty that this place has to offer.

"This place is amazing," I tell him with a smile on my lips.

"You get used to it." He shrugs after a while.

"You've got to be the richest person I know," I tell him in utter disbelief of everything that I'm looking at. Sure, I know that he has fashion sense and style, but I didn't expect him to be this rich. I didn't expect him to own an actual estate. That's what this is called right? An estate. I look at it with a baffled, bewildered curiosity, wondering what everything has to hold.

That's when I see all the gorgeous, glamorous, and attractive people who are wandering around the front of the mansion, letting valets take their cars away. They walk in the finest dresses and tuxedos that I've ever seen. Smiling and laughing with each other, I suddenly feel like I'm completely under-dressed, looking at all the other people that I'll be competing with for Roman's attention. I should have thought this through. I should have dressed in something else. I close my eyes and shake my head.

"I'm way under-dressed," I tell him with a worried tone in my voice.

"No you're not," he laughs. "You look incredible. Don't worry a second about how you look."

I feel a sinking feeling deep inside my stomach. This is a mistake. He pulls up to the doorway where a valet immediately rushes to open his door for him. I watch Roman step out gracefully as a valet opens my door as well. I look at him and wonder what kind of a man he truly is. His history and past suddenly seem so dark and mysterious to me. I want to crack him open and take a look inside at what he has hidden away.

He walks around the car and offers me his arm. I take it gratefully, feeling like he's my shield against everything crazy that the night is bound to hold for me. We approach the doors cautiously, greeted by people whom I assume are servants wearing masks, stretching their arms out, guiding us into the house. I feel like we're being funneled in toward the pulsing music beating through my skin and into my heart, pounding and coaxing my heart to follow. I walk past the masked faces, looking at us as we walk.

Glancing over at Roman, I see he's holding a mask in his left hand. From where I stand, it looks like a black wolf's face.

When we enter the house, I'm completely floored by the stylish lighting, the marble, ornate patterns on the floor. It's dimly lit, looking more like a club than an actual mansion. It's not what I expected at all. I was thinking that there would be an orchestra or at least strings playing in the background. Not club music. Looking at Roman, I watch as he pulls on his wolf's face. I like it. It suits him.

"Give me one second," Roman says to me with a smile on his lips. "I have to tell someone that I'm here."

I watch him walk away, feeling lonely, abandoned, and isolated. There are so many people around me, talking and laughing with one another that I feel like I'm a sore thumb, sticking out from the crowd as they all wash over me, a boulder in the stream. I have no idea where Roman has gone but I do know that I'm completely alone right now. I feel like I should be doing something, walking somewhere or talking to someone, but I have no clue what that is.

"You look lost." A man wearing a mask that looks very similar to Roman's approaches me. His bright blue eyes look at me with bold intensity. At first, I think he works here, searching for people that need help or are lost. I look at him with a smile and shake my head.

"I'm just waiting for someone," I tell him with a sheepish look on

my face.

The man looks at me. His eyes are as cold and unforgiving as ice. As I look at them behind the black mask, I feel as though I'm looking upon a frozen alpine lake, bitter and lonely, isolated for a reason. Jagged shards of ice sticking up, hateful and spiteful toward others who are not welcome. The man does not look like he should be left unattended, for everyone's safety.

"Don't get lost then," he tells me in a low, rumbling voice as he turns and looks at the other guests. "This house is easy to get lost in, little rabbit."

Before I can respond with something witty about having great navigational skills, he turns and walks away, sinking into the flock of people passing through the house. I try to watch him go, but he's long gone before I can say a word to him.

"Hey, you." I feel Roman's hand on my wrist as he turns me around and smiles at me, holding a glass of what I assume to be champagne in his other hand.

"Care for a bit of courage?" he asks me with a chuckle.

I take it from him eagerly, willing to have something that will help me out here. If there are going to be more, other people, like that last man, then I'm going to need something. I take a long drink and I can hear Roman laughing at the sight while I down half of the champagne glass. I look at him bitterly, but there's no way I could be angry at him. He's too cute.

"Come on," he says, taking my hand. "I'll give you the grand tour."

Roman takes me through the crowd, cutting through them with skilled precision and artful talent. It seems that he's done this before. As he walks through the doorway into a slightly less crowded room and then through another doorway, I feel like we're going somewhere we shouldn't be. Eventually, as each room thins more and more, we come to a point where we're all alone, walking down a hallway. Eventually, I have to ask him.

"What do your parents do?" I ask him finally, unable to believe all the rooms we're passing.

"They're in acquisitions," Roman says with a shrug, like it's nothing. "They invest in a lot of businesses, scout people who can help them with their needs. They're very hands-on with their employees. But over all, they just dabble successfully in a lot of stuff."

"Wouldn't I love to just dabble successfully in stuff," I say bitterly, looking around at everything they have. "They made all of this?"

"Oh, no." Roman shakes his head. "They've inherited most of it. My family is old world wealth. They came to America to colonize and ended up transferring over here. Sort of the American dream back in the day."

"That must be cool," I tell him, "to have all that history."

"It's okay," he says dismissively. "It's a lot of expectations and seriousness. There aren't a lot of laughs and good times to be had when the parties aren't happening."

"A shame," I say as he stops in front of a door. "What's this?" I ask him, looking at the deep colors of the wooden door. He grins at me, even though I think I have a pretty good idea of what it is.

He throws open the door to his room and I look inside at how incredibly stylish and nice it is. This isn't the kind of room that you'd expect a former youth to occupy. It's full of blacks and greys and teals. I look at it and smile, it's the kind of room I would expect Roman to have, even as a young boy.

"I put in my hellos," he says to me, finally. "We could go mingle downstairs with a bunch of stodgy businessmen and their trophy wives, or we could hang out up here and bide our time."

I smile at him, taking another sip of my champagne. "You have more of this?" I ask him.

"There's an entertainment room down the hall," he says with a shrug. "There's a full mini bar and fridge in there." He points to where the door to the entertainment room is. "After everyone's drunk enough, we can pop back down for a second before heading home."

"Sounds good with me," I tell him, leaning in and feeling our masks clacking together as our lips meet, passionately welcoming each other back.

*

Somewhere between watching Conan on TV and talking with him, I'm not sure when I started kissing him. I'm not sure either of us knows. I pull back, looking at him and I can't help but feel like I'm kissing a man with many secrets.

What I've been able to put together about Roman's life, I'm able to stuff into a thimble. The sight of Roman is enough to make me melt, but in the end, I know so little about him. It hurts to think about how much he could be hiding from me, how much he is hiding from me. A man with this much money and this much history in his past has to have secrets. I know that those secrets come back to haunt those in relationships.

I kiss him again, my lips locking with his and feeling the power of his body rippling through me. It's something that makes me tingle and tickle all over. I hold him close, my fingers on his back, keeping his body close to me.

Everything about him is mysterious and exciting, something that I should be worried about, something that I should monitor, but I don't. I don't hold back with him. As we kiss, he moves away from my lips, kissing my keeps, softly pressing his lips to my skin and making me want to squeal with excitement.

"Your body is amazing," he whispers into my ear as I feel his hands on my side. His fingers are strong, tough, the kind of hands that convey the power in them. I smile at the sensation of him holding my body, of him appreciating my body. I've worked hard on my body, the way I've dedicated myself to training, working out, and dressing. I've been dedicated to the way I've worked out over the years. Since I was in college, I have been spending hours every week at the gym. He kisses my neck and I run my hands over his stomach. "You're perfect," he says to me.

"You're not so bad yourself," I say to him, feeling his musculature, wanting him all over. I feel his biceps, his shoulders, everything seems like it's so toned and hardened from everything he's done himself. I feel his hands gripping just under my breast. God, I want him to go all the way. I want him to have me, to go for me with everything he has. It feels primal inside of me, something potent, screaming to come out. His hands continue to explore me, searching and hunting all over me.

His hand reaches up and grips my breast and I feel the strength of his fingers. I let out a gasp as he feels my breast, finding that I'm not wearing a bra. I smile as he grins, closing his eyes in euphoria. I let his hands sneak up, touching the top of my breasts, bare from the dress. His fingers hook into the cloth of the dress and pull it down, letting the cool air kiss my breasts, cooling my nipples. His hands immediately grip my breasts, massaging them and making me feel like I'm in heaven right now. He tweaks my nipples, squeezing them as he works. I feel completely blissful. He cups my breast, leaning in and kissing my nipple, sucking on it. I feel it between his lips, I feel him sucking on it, tickling me. I smile, letting out a sigh of excitement.

His free hand slowly runs down my dress, feeling the skin of my stomach, reaching deeper and running his fingers over the wet lips of my vagina. I let out a gasp as he causes me to shudder, just with the feeling of his fingers on me. He gets bolder, running his fingers over me again as he sucks on my other nipple, circling it with his tongue, kissing it gently, and sucking on it. I lean back on the bed, feeling his swollen penis over his pants as he rubs my clit. I arch my back, grinding my pelvis into his hand, begging him silently for more. He obliges me, working his hand over me, sending shocks of excitement through my body. I want to scream, but I keep it quiet, not wanting to draw attention to us up here. He slips his fingers inside of me and I let out a moan, begging for more.

Finally, I get his belt undone and hook my fingers under his pants and underwear, forcing them down in one push and unleashing his cock. I watch it fall out and smile at the sight of it. Wrapping my fingers around it, I feel how stiff it is, how hot it is. It feels like I'm gripping a living furnace. Squeezing it, I watch his whole body shake as he kisses between my breasts, immersing his face in between them.

"Fuck me," I tell him. "Stop playing around and fuck me."

"Such a lady," he teases, pulling my dress and underwear off obediently. I laugh at the feeling of being naked. Unbuttoning his shirt, I feel the tip of his penis on my stomach, teasing me. When he's completely naked as well, I grip his shoulders and throw him down on the bed. I like to be in control. I like to be on top. He gazes up at me, staring in disbelief as I drop down onto his stomach, rocking back and forth, seeing how he likes to be teased. I look at his face, full of excitement and passion as he looks up at me. Behind me, my ass rubs against his swollen cock. I reach back and stroke it, keeping it rigid for me.

Pushing myself up, I hold his cock, guiding him into me. His tip touches my lips and I feel like I've been struck by lightning and with every inch that he pushes inside of me, I feel like I'm going to die from the excitement and the pleasure of all of it. As he slips deeper and deeper inside of me, I throw back my head and gasp, taking him all in. When he sinks all the way in and I'm all the way down, I gently rock back and forth, watching him as his hands grip my thighs, holding on for the ride. All across his face are etched the signs of pure delight. I gasp again, feeling like someone is stabbing me with pure ecstasy.

Rocking back and forth, the feeling of him inside of me is like a sword of fire. My breathing picks up, quickening and as he begins to pull in and out, thrusting himself into me, I lean forward and kiss him, my nipples rubbing against his chest. He keeps fucking me, harder and harder as his hands grip my neck, holding me close. Finally, he pushes me back, throwing me onto the bed and lifting my legs.

I look up at him as I wrap my legs around his back, his cock diving inside of me, pushing again and again. I grip the bed frame, moaning and groaning in euphoria as he continues to push inside and pull out. Finally, I've hit it where I don't think I can take it anymore. It's too much, too perfect. I feel like I'm full of light. Gripping my legs, he holds me close, pushing himself deep inside of me as he cums, throwing back his head and letting out a groan of his own. I smile at the sight of it, feeling completely overwhelmed with pure enjoyment.

When he drops down onto the bed, I look at him, feeling tingly inside as the warmth of his cum fills me. I want to pass out from the euphoria that grips me, shaking me and causing my entire body to tingle. I look over at him as he lays down next to me, breathing just as heavily as I am, a smile written across his lips and in his eyes. He loved it, just as much as I did.

There's a knock on the door and I feel my heart nearly jump out of my chest. I look over at Roman whose grin is fading away quickly. Glaring, he quickly slips on his suit's pants and makes his way toward the door, shirtless. I can hardly see what is going on from the bed and as I look at him, I feel nervous. All I can think about is his family. What if they want to talk to him? What if they want to pass through the door and have a quick chat with him and I'm in here, naked on his bed like some sort of slut?

When he closes the door, I'm already slipping on my underwear. His eyes are on me as he approaches me, but I have nothing to say to him right now. That was incredible and I don't want to ruin the moment by wasting words on him. In a moment, there's never been a more perfect thing to me than what I've done with him. I know how things are with his family. There's nothing he needs to say. I know how this is going to go.

"Sorry," Roman says to me calmly. "My father is asking for me."

"Oh," I say to him, guessing right. Suddenly, I feel sick, like I've drank too much. I look at him and see him smiling at me.

"You look so beautiful," he says to me, sitting on the edge of the bed and kissing my shoulder. I smile at the tingling sensation of his lips on my skin. Every time he touches me, I feel better. I feel like I'm the best when he touches me. He watches me as I slip my dress back on and I can feel his eyes devouring every inch of my body.

"Are you alright?" he asks me. I can feel him reading me, picking up the details of my emotions, just from my body language.

"I'm fine," I say to him, cringing at my use of the word fine. He's going to pick up on that immediately. He's going to know that I'm not fine. "I'm just feeling a little under the weather," I confess to him, knowing that it's going to sound like a lie when he hears it.

"Are you okay?" He asks me. "Is there anything I can do for you?"

I shake my head. "I think it might have been something I ate," I tell him.

Honestly, I think it's probably the opposite. I haven't eaten a thing today. I'm looking at over twenty four hours since I've had anything substantial to eat. Maybe if I just go home and have something to eat, I'll be better. Or maybe if I go downstairs, I'll be able to find something to eat and I'll feel better.

I'm fully dressed in another minute while Roman is watching me as he dresses himself. When I'm done, I look down at the white rabbit mask, dotted with diamonds. I can't take that home. As I look at it, I feel repulsed by it. This isn't me. I don't have sex with guys I've only known for a few days. As I make my way toward the door, Roman reaches out and takes my hand.

"There's a driver who will take you home," Roman says solemnly. There's pain and worry in his eyes, I don't know why. I find it strange that he would look so emotional. "Do you mind if I call you tomorrow?" he asks me. "I have to go speak with my father. It may take a while. If you don't mind sticking around, I'll drive you home, myself."

"You can call me tomorrow," I say to him, offering him a smile. "I'm going to just head home, take some Nyquil, and then go to sleep."

I turn and head through the entrance as he smiles at me, letting me go. I feel worse with each step, feeling sicker and sicker as I step away from him.

Passing through the mob, I feel sick, lost and slightly disoriented. Walking, trying not to stumble, I feel something inside of me, something that makes me nauseous. I've just had the best sex of my life, but I feel like I've just downed an entire bottle of whiskey.

Swaying as I walk, I feel like I'm going to throw up. All around me, lights flash and music pulses, pounding deep inside of me. It makes me feel worse, like all the world is a surreal dream. I look at the faces around me, masked and shrouded in a dozen different animals, all looking and turning to face me.

Their eyes are harsh, staring at me with bright intensity. All of their eyes look so severe, so bold as they watch me. Inside of me, I feel like there's something they all know that I don't. As I walk, I feel like my knees are going to give out and I'm going to collapse. God, I wish I wasn't wearing these heels.

"Are you lost?" the wolf asks me again as I go toward the atrium. He's standing by a black column, staring at me with his arms crossed, his bold blue eyes watching me with hungry intensity.

"I'm fine," I say to him with a half-smile. "Thank you," I say bitterly, avoiding him and walking through the far side of the hall. I'm making my way toward the entrance where the dozens of servants are all standing, hands folded behind their backs. I look at them as I pass them. Looking at the door, I turn to one of the servants, feeling like I'm going to throw up.

The whole world feels like its swirling and churning around me. Everything is going to shatter if I stop moving. I need to get out of here. I need to get away from all of them.

"Can someone call me a taxi?" I say to the nearest servant.

"Absolutely, miss," the nearest servant says to me. He stretches his hand out toward the entrance. "There's a driver who will take you home."

I don't remember getting to the car. I don't even remember getting into it or the driver talking to me. When I wake up in my bed, I feel cold, sick, and alone. All around me, the darkness of the house makes me feel like I'm not alone. I roll over in my bed, looking out the window at the illuminated street, drenched in pale, neon light from the streetlights. It's quiet out there. I don't see a soul out on the street. My fingers and hands are shaking. I need to eat something, maybe. I'm not sure what's wrong with me, but I feel wrong.

Is there someone out there watching me with cold eyes? I feel sick all over, inside and out. There's something wrong. I turn and barely make it to the bathroom before I throw up. There's nothing inside of me to throw up, but I don't bother looking inside the toilet. Wiping my lips, I flush the toilet and walk turn to look at myself in the mirror. I'm still wearing the dress I wore to the party. How did I get here? I don't understand.

* * *

In the morning, I wake to the sound of the alarm screaming in my face. Peeling open my eyes, I look at it with hatred and bitterness. I feel like it's assaulted everything about the natural order of things. Shutting it off, I feel the soft, relief of silence washing over me. The familiar sounds of the city sneak in through the windows like bandits. I smile at their arrival. Everything seems better right now.

Pushing up from the bed and throwing my covers off, I see that at some point in the night I changed clothes. I don't remember when. I look at myself in the mirror, deciding that it's time to get ready. I don't have time to stand around and think about how royally screwed up last night was. No, I need to get ready. I have a shift in less than an hour. I make my way to the bathroom and quickly get showered. After a while, I look at myself in the mirror and see how pale and sickly I look. I can feel the sickness swirling in my stomach.

My usual breakfast of yogurt and eggs doesn't work with me. I feel my stomach churning and swirling. I can feel it lunging and jumping inside of my stomach and I quickly rush to the bathroom. I barely make it over the toilet before I throw up again. I try to get myself together and make my way out of the house. Locking up the door as

I go, I walk down the stairs and toward my car. Standing in front of it, I click the button and watch the lights flash in the early morning light.

Before I get into car, I look around, feeling the hairs on the back of my neck standing up, the same way they felt last night when I looked out of my bedroom window. Glancing up to my window on the second floor, I see my closed blinds and try to pinpoint where the feeling came from down here. I feel slightly brave in the daylight hours, but then again, I only feel slightly braver. The terror still pounds in my heart and my churning stomach isn't helping me. I glance around, expecting to see some sort of shadowy figure lurking just beyond my sight, but there's nothing here.

Dropping into the car, I slip the keys into the ignition and twist, feeling my car groaning to life. As I make my way toward the hotel, I barely notice the man standing by the street corner. But then, I instantly recognize him as the man from yesterday, who was at the bar, staring at my car while he talked on his cell phone.

Now, his cold, blue eyes watch me as I drive away. I feel a tremor rippling down my spine as I catch sight of him.

CHAPTER FOUR

I keep my eyes on the front entrance for most of the morning, watching from the office, trying to hide from anyone who might enter the hotel. Looking at the doorway, I feel more and more sick with each passing hour. I don't know what I'm looking for, maybe Roman, maybe the man who was at the bar. There's nothing about this that makes me feel good. I can't function like this. As I look around for any sign of the man, I realize that I need to take the rest of the day off and go home.

"You look horrible," Desire says to me with a smile on her face. "Was it that great of a night?"

I look at her. No, I glare at her. I'm not in the mood for games right now.

"I don't remember a lot of it," I say to her with a weak smile on my face. Desire glances at me, chewing on her lips, as Maria turns and looks at me with a sympathetic look on her face.

"Did he do anything to you?" Maria asks me.

"No," I assure her solemnly. "It's fine. I just woke up sick. I think I have food poisoning."

"Did you eat anything there?" Maria asks me, suddenly worried.

"No, it must have been something before," I shake my head.

"You should go home," Desire says to me. "If you're not feeling good, I don't want you getting all your ickyness around me. You should take the day and get out of here. Drink some tea and binge watch something on Netflix."

"Thanks, Dez," I say bitterly.

In the end, I feel like I might have something worth doing when I think about going home. I can relax, try and get over whatever it is that's bothering me. I look back into the office and know that if I leave, Desire and Maria are here to man the ramparts.

Staring out at the front, I'm expecting at any moment to see the man from the bar at the glass. There's nothing waiting out there, nothing staring back at me.

Turning around, I go into the office and grab my coat and purse. There's nothing outside to make me think that I'm being followed, but I can't shake the feeling. I feel like there's madness spider webs clinging to me. I look around for the source, but it feels like it's all over. There's just insanity all over.

"Okay," I tell them as I step out of the office, trying to get away from everything. "I'm going to go home early, drink some tea, and binge watch something on Netflix."

"Good for you," Desire says to me. "Now get out of here."

"Feel better," Maria wishes me as I go.

As I make my way across the lobby, I let Bernie open the door for me. When I go out, I give Bernie a nod, smiling to him as he says farewell to me. I look at him as he grins at me with his big Santa Claus smile that covers him from ear to ear. I walk past him, feeling the pale light on me. It's not warm. It's not welcoming. It's just a cold lie today. I walk through the light, heading for my car.

Rounding the Chateau, I look at where I usually park, where I always park. I stop the moment I spot my car. Standing right next to it, looking in through the driver's window, the man in the suit with the cell phone is standing right next to it, glaring at something.

I look at the man, standing in his dark coat, a fedora on his head and his dark brown hair peeking out from the back of his hat. I notice that he's wearing black leather gloves, the kind that you'd expect a man with piano wire to wear right before murdering someone. I take a deep breath and step backwards. I don't know why he's there.

What could he possibly want with me? I turn and start to make my way in the opposite direction, praying that he doesn't turn around and find me hurrying the other way. I look at Bernie who is standing at the door, looking at me questioningly. I offer him a friendly wave, trying to assure him that I'm not going in the wrong direction by accident. I don't want him shouting at me or calling my name affectionately. He waves at me with a big toothy grin. As I go, he looks at me without a care or worry in the world.

As I walk, I try to figure out what the next move in my plan should be. I can't just wander around without a clue as to what I'm going to do. No, I need a plan. I need an objective to start working toward. I don't want him finding me. This is the third time that I've seen him. Why is he following me? As I keep walking, I try to figure out what he's doing chasing after me. It's not like I've got some great, dark secret for him to uncover. I have nothing to do with him or anything that would be of interest to the likes of him.

I stop, frozen in place. Looking around, I know why this guy is chasing after me. It's Roman. The moment Roman appeared inside the lobby and I had drinks with him was the moment that man started appearing. I suddenly feel like I've been right about my paranoia, about someone watching me. This man following me has something to do with Roman. After all, if there's something unique or mysterious in my life right now, it's Roman. He came out of nowhere, swept me off my feet and has taken me on a whirlwind romance before all of this strange madness started. I look over my shoulder toward the corner of the parking lot that I can still see. I can't see the man, but I know he's still there.

Who is he talking to? As I turn back and start walking, I notice a woman in tan boots and a long white coat coming toward me. She's wearing a large white hat and enormous sunglasses that cover her eyes, and cheeks. Her lips are painted in bold, vivid red lipstick. As she walks toward me, I think that I should get a hat and some sunglasses as well, hide myself so that the man following won't notice me. As I approach her, I notice that she's wearing white gloves as well, talking on her phone with a great red smile on her lips.

"Claire?" she says as I draw closer to her. I notice immediately that she's not from around here. In fact, she sounds like she's Russian or Eastern European. I look at her, stopping as I walk, feeling like I've been hit with a brick. "Claire, my dear, is that you?" she asks, hanging up her phone.

"I'm sorry," I say to her, shaking my head, worrying that the mysterious stalker might come after me at any second. "You must be mistaken."

"No, not at all," she says to me with that enormous smile on her lips. "I would recognize you anywhere." She slips her phone into her pocket and tilts her head slightly, as if she's examining me from behind those enormous lenses of hers.

"You're positively marvelous, aren't you?"

"I don't know who you are," I say to her. "You'll have to forgive me."

"Of course you don't know who I am," she says, reaching out and gently touching me on the arm. "Now, Claire, it's vitally important that you listen to me. You're going to need to do exactly as I say or Bartrand is going to be very unpleasant with you."

"Who is Bartrand?" I ask her.

"The man standing behind you," she says to me.

Instantly I turn around and look into the cold, arctic blue eyes of the man who was looking into my car. Suddenly, I realize that I've run into this man more than once. In fact, I recognize him from the party last night with Roman. He was the other wolf, the one that kept asking me if I was lost and warning me to be careful. I look at him as he stares at me with a sort of hunger that makes my skin crawl. He looks like he wants to hurt me or rough me up a bit, like he's the kind of man that gets off on that. He reaches up and taps the rim of his fedora, as if he's introducing himself to me wordlessly.

"I don't understand," I tell them both, taking a step away from both

of them.

"We know," the woman says to me as a car pulls out of traffic and comes to the sidewalk. It's jet black, the kind of dark black that you'd expect midnight to look like if someone pierced it and it started to bleed. "You look so pale, my dear. Come with us. We'll take you somewhere nice, make you feel better."

I watch as Bartrand opens the door to the car, offering me the seat in the back. The woman, elegant, beautiful, and as lovely as a white rose, makes her way to the opposite side of the car. "I'm not going with you," I tell her bluntly.

"You don't have a choice, dear," she says to me with a purring, beautiful voice like chocolate and velvet.

She's right. I know that she's right. I take a step toward the door that Bartrand is holding open for me. He looks at me with his cold, unnerving eyes and doesn't say a word to me. I am lost now. I'm completely lost and I know that if he tells me not to get lost that I'm going to freak out on him and claw his eyes out. I didn't ask for this. I didn't want this. All I wanted was to fall in love with a man who was perfect and grow old with him. Why has everything gone so completely insane all of a sudden?

On the car ride, all I can do is listen as the woman next to me talks into her phone, laughing occasionally and glancing over at me. I have no clue what she's saying or what language she's even speaking. While she talks, I'm given ample opportunity to freak out and panic over the path that has lead me to this point. I don't know what I was expecting, but this wasn't it. I wanted something better than this. I have my cell phone with me. I could call the cops. I could call Maria or Desire or anyone to come and rescue me. I don't have to take this sitting down. I can fight.

But as the car makes its way through the city, climbing out of the urban sprawl and into a part of the city that grows greener and greener with each passing mile, I suddenly have a sense of where we are and where we're going. I look out the window and see that we're heading back toward the mansion, back toward the world that I thought I'd put behind myself last night. I feel sick, like I'm going to throw up.

"Keep it together, dear," the woman says to me. "We're almost

there."

"I want to go home," I tell her bluntly, trying to grasp some courage.

It's only fifteen more minutes and we're at the estate that I had been so impressed with the night before. I look around at all of the statues and the opulent carvings that had impressed me in the luminous glory of the party and see them through a new haunting light. I see wolves everywhere I look, carved in with the humans, chasing, hunting, snarling, and clawing. I didn't notice them last night, but now, in the light of day, it's so obvious. They're clearly obsessed with wolves.

The car comes to a stop and I stare with utter disbelief as Bartrand steps out of the front door and approaches the car, opening the door for me and extending a hand.
I look at him, wondering how in the world he got here faster than we did. The driver must have drawn out the journey so that he could make his way here before us.

I follow the woman in white as she walks with familiar comfort through the front door and into the enormous, immaculate mansion, tossing her hat, sunglasses, gloves, and coat to the nearest servant. I notice that she's wearing a beautiful white dress and walks with such grace and poise that it makes me envious.

'Claire," she says as we enter a long, ornately crafted and decorated room with a crackling fireplace and high backed furniture for guests to sit in waiting for us. "Allow me to introduce you to Rufus and Loraine, the patriarch and matriarch of our clan. They are your beloved and welcoming guests for this afternoon."

I see a man rise in such regally fancy attire that I immediately know that he is the man Roman addressed as his father from the stories I was told. Everything from the velvet jacket to the silk ascot, the man's silver beard and charcoal hair is exactly like Roman described.

Next to him is an extremely young looking lady with deep auburn hair that hangs over her shoulders in thick, luscious curls. She looks at me with pink lips and bright eyes, welcoming me. She gives the white rose woman a run for her money in the looks department. They're both exquisite figures and standards for women everywhere to envy.

"Welcome to our home, Claire," Rufus says to me in a deep, rumbling voice. "Roman has told us much about you."

"So this is about Roman," I say bluntly. "Do you send your goon and daughter to collect all of his girlfriends?"

"Only the special ones," Loraine says with a chuckle. "Svetlana is not our daughter, but more of a family friend. This is the estate belonging to the Clan of the Wolf, a proud estate that has stood tall since the founding of this nation. We'd like to extend an invitation to you, Claire. You are an extremely rare young woman."

"We have a secret, Claire," Rufus says, stretching out his hand, motioning me for a seat. I begrudgingly take it. Walking over to the seat, I sit down and look across the coffee table at Rufus and Loraine who sit so properly. Svetlana, the white rose, sits in a chair farthest away from the coffee table. I look at her as she seems completely disinterested in the events unfolding in front of us.

I look at Rufus and feel like I'm going to throw up. God, why do I keep getting sick?

"Roman, Svetlana, Loraine, Bartrand, and I are all what we lovingly call shifters."

I look at him, completely distant, not sure what the hell I just heard.

"What?"

"We're shifters," he repeats. "We're an old world clan. Most of us are werewolves, but some of us have more unique and diverse talents available at our disposal. It's a rare thing to be a shifter, something beautiful and powerful. It may be hard for you to grasp this, but we're an ancient order of mythical entities. We're not used to showing ourselves to outsiders, but we're willing to make an exception to you."

"This is bullshit," I tell him, shaking my head. "You have no proof."

"We have proof," Loraine tells me. "You see, it's hard for shifters to reproduce. Having children is nearly impossible for us, it's a sort of natural system of checks and balances to ensure that we don't take over the world or something like that." She laughs at the absurdity of it all. I look at them, not buying it at all.

"As for you, Roman has found you to be compatible for our condition. In other words, you're capable of giving birth to the next generation of shifters."

"I'm leaving now," I tell them.

"Feeling sick, darling?" Rufus asks me before I can stand up. "Throwing up a little? Sweating? Are you having a hard time grasping reality from fantasy? All signs of the accelerated pregnancy that comes with our culture. If you need proof that what we say is real, you're going to want to see a doctor and have an ultrasound. You'll see all the proof you need."

"You're lying," I tell him, knowing all too well that he's not. I've never been pregnant before, but I just watched Chloe go through all of it. I know the signs. I've wanted a baby for so long that I've known everything about the process. Since he said that I am pregnant, I've known that my symptoms are exact. I feel like I'm going to throw up. This can't be true.

"Roman has had the good fortune of being first to you," Rufus says coldly across the coffee table to me. "It's a fortune that he will only have. We operate in a pack system here. After you have given birth to the next generation of the Clan of the Wolf's first member, you'll have relations with me. A bit primal and barbaric sounding, I know, but the rules are boldly concrete. So there you have it."

"Don't worry about me," Loraine says with a strange, bright smile. "I understand completely. Don't expect any jealousy from any of us. We all enjoy the company of Rufus. You'll be welcomed in fully and completely."

"I'm leaving," I tell him resolutely.

"I'm sorry, darling," Rufus says coldly.

As I stand, I instantly realize that Bartrand is standing behind me. I can't go. It's not an option for me to just get up and leave this house. I have to stay. I'm not given a choice. If what they're telling me is true, then I'm their prisoner here. I'm not going to be able to escape.

"But we've already set up a room for you," Rufus said. "You're such a treasure, that we can't risk losing you. Until we've completed our work, you're going to need to stay with us."

"I'm your prisoner?" I say coldly.

"I'm sorry, Claire," I hear Roman say behind me and close my eyes.

Oh God, what have I gotten into? I close my eyes and feel the world crushing all around me. I can't go back now. I can't go back to my old life. I'm stuck here. I can feel the tears welling up in my eyes.

CHAPTER FIVE

This isn't a dream. God, I wish it were. The more I sit here, thinking, the more I know that it's absolute madness. The more I want to scream and shout and to pretend that none of this is real. But with each passing second, the more I know that it is real. I know that it's not something they all went in on to make me look like a fool. No, it's true. But how?

How can shifters be a real thing?

I was never into the horror stories or fairy tale lovers' movements. When I was little, I never thought about werewolves or monsters like that, even around Halloween. I always thought that they were stupid, pointless and there was nothing interesting about them. In fact, when they revamped the whole genre with movies and books, they looked dumber than ever to me.

How is this real? How could there be any truth to these folktales and superstitions? No, this has to be some sick and twisted family prank. They're messing with me. They're jerks and they want to get inside of my head, and the poor girls were their victims. What am I doing here still?

But more important than that, they expect me to believe that I'm pregnant? But, like them telling me that they're shifters, I know that they're telling the truth. I've felt wrong, sick, and different since I had sex with Roman. I don't know why and I thought it might be food poisoning, but the moment they told me that I was pregnant, it sort of clicked inside of me.

My God, I'm pregnant.

Not only am I pregnant, but I'm pregnant with a lunatic's baby. How am I supposed to explain that to everyone I know? Actually, how in the world am I going to be able to go back to that world? I look around at the opulent room I'm stuck in with Roman's lecherous father and his harem of women. They expect me to be one of them? They expect me to just be okay with all of this? My hands are trembling. There's something wrong. I think I'm going into shock. How am I supposed to handle all of this?

"I'm sorry, Claire." I hear his voice and it fills me with rage. I want to take a swing at his stupid, handsome face. I want to cave it in with a single blow. I should grab a fire poker from the fireplace and stick it in his eye. But more importantly, I have some questions that I need answered first, like how come my birth control didn't protect me from him. Why didn't it stop me from getting pregnant with their demon baby?

Slowly, I turn around and look at Roman who is standing in the doorway, leaning against the frame with his arms crossed, looking down at his shoes. What a bastard and a coward. He won't even look at me. He doesn't have the balls to stand up to his father and he didn't have the balls to tell me all of this himself. There's no way I could ever fall for a man like him.

"Am I a prisoner here?" I ask Rufus, ignoring Roman.

I can feel Bartrand's eyes on me, like serpents slithering. It's almost as if he's a hungry dog, waiting for a bone. Rufus, sitting in his lavish, wealthy clothes, glances at Loraine and Svetlana who are flanking him like perfect, unblemished statues. They meet his gaze for a second before turning back to me, staring at me with clear, thoughtful eyes.

"We'd like to consider you a guest," Rufus says to me in his deep, gruff voice. "After all, you are a very prized and valuable asset that we don't want to lose. The world is a dangerous place, Claire. We don't want to risk some accident befalling you and ripping you from us too soon. Here, you'll have all the luxury you could imagine, a serving staff waiting on you hand and foot, and all the security you could possibly need."

"From accidents?" I lift an eyebrow. "Sounds like being a prisoner to me."

"Only in a negative light dear," Svetlana says to me in her purring voice. "The Clan of the Wolf is a very powerful and influential family here. There's nowhere you can escape to where we won't have eyes and ears. Do you want to spend the rest of your life looking over your shoulder, wondering if Bartrand is a few feet away from you?"

I sit there a moment, understanding completely. If it's so rare for a woman to be able to give birth to a Shifter and I'm one of those precious few, then I know that they're not going to let me go. They're going to follow me and shadow me no matter where I go in this life. I have to be smart about this. I have to know what I'm doing or they're going to kill me once they're done with me.

"So I'm nothing more than a baby factory for you?" I look at Rufus coldly. Of course, the child growing inside of me is Roman's, but the rest, those are going to be Rufus's. He made that abundantly clear when he told me about this. I'm not interested in being his baby maker.

Rufus lords around this mansion with his harem of Shifter women, having sex with each of them and claiming them as his own while the men lurk in the shadows, waiting for their turn. I think about Roman and Bartrand, wondering how many others there are like them and how many others are out there like Svetlana, smiling as he uses them for his own twisted, sick desires. I'm not okay with that. I'm not okay with that at all.

"You are the vessel of the future," Rufus declares passionately, as if that's supposed to mean something to me. It's not some sacred honor that has been bestowed upon me. No. I'm forced to do this and I don't want to have any part of it. "You will usher in a new generation of the Clan of the Wolf, something that has not happened in a very long time. This will give our clan the unique opportunity of superiority. This will put us ahead of all others. You will be honored and respected as the one who is responsible for this and you will be treated according to the honor bestowed upon you."

I look at him, harvesting everything that he's saying to me. I don't know if this is some sort of sick game or not, but I'm not going to be a victim in all of it. I have to keep fighting. I have to keep trying to find a way out of this. I feel my hand running over my stomach, thinking about the life inside of me.

If I am pregnant, I don't want that child to be a part of this life. I don't want that child to be locked in some sort of sick fantasy world with the likes of Rufus to teach him how to survive, how to learn all that life has to offer. I won't be a pawn in their games. I'm not that kind of person. I'm not going to have my life be dictated by these freaks.

"Am I allowed to go home?" I ask them, trying to keep my calm. I could try to run, that much I know. I could try and make a break for it and see if I can survive on my own before Bartrand and Roman hunt me down.

"If you want," Rufus tells me, stroking his sable beard, watching my every move with his haunting eyes. "But you'll need to accept that we'll be sending an escort with you. Claire, you need to accept some hard truths. I know we're asking a lot from you right now, but it's only because your survival greatly depends upon it.

"There are other clans who will try to take advantage of you and they will not be nearly as friendly as I have been with you. But let us be clear about one last thing, Claire. We cannot allow you to fall into enemy hands. Betray us or run away from us and we'll be forced to take extreme measures with you."

I don't need a translator. I got that loud and clear. It feels like someone stuck a boulder in my stomach. I'm trying to be brave, but it's hard right now. Everything suddenly got too crazy for me. I want out. I want to escape all of this, but I know that I can't just run away. I have to fight. I have to stay alive. Especially if they're threatening things like killing me, I have to stay alert and strong.

"Fine," I tell him. "I just want to get a few things."

"We'll take care of any other concerns you might have," Loraine says in her sweet, songbird voice. It's the kind of voice that makes my heart shrivel with what it's hiding deep down inside. "It'll be a smooth transition for you. Seamless."

I offer her a tentative smile, but that's all I can give her at the moment. I slowly rise and feel like I'm going to throw up. Oh, that feeling, I'm so glad that it's returned to me. It's something that I have been missing for the past twenty minutes or so. Looking around, I see that Bartrand is standing right behind me, as gruff and grim as ever. Roman is still at the door, pretending like he hasn't betrayed me in the worst possible way.

"Bartrand will see that you make it home and back safely," Rufus says to me in a low, sinister voice. He clearly doesn't trust me. Smart. If he did trust me, then I would be to Canada or Mexico before he had a clue. I make my way toward the door, tentatively looking at Roman as I walk by him, refusing to give him the satisfaction of a single word. He's not worthy of any of them.

Bartrand follows me like a shadow as we make our way back through the house. I look around at the maids cleaning and the servants going about their business. I wonder how many of them are Shifters, how many of them know what's going on at this house. Is there anyone here that has a clue or are they all in on it? Maybe they're all shifters and they all have these strange understandings of what their place is inside their strange clan.

I look at them as they glance up at me with worried and curious eyes. They know. They have to know. This whole clan thing is operating like some sort of sick pack. Is this normal? Of course it's not. What am I saying?

Outside another car is just now pulling up, dark navy and glossy as all the other cars I've seen outside this mansion. A man steps out from behind the wheel with feathery brown hair and a smile the size of the moon. He's wearing sunglasses, but he reminds me of a less stern and less severe looking. He has a boyish playfulness that catches me off guard with Bartrand's dark, looming cloud hanging over head.

"Is this her?" he asks me. "By the Wolf, it's her."

"Pipe down, Remi," Bartrand growls, that same voice that I remember from the party. There's nothing unfamiliar about him. I feel like the past few days, I've been stuck with him lingering over my shoulder. "Get out of the way," he snarls at Remi, clearly another member of their pack.

"Justine, are you seeing this?" he asks as the passenger door opens. I watch as a slender red head moves out of the car. She is perfectly aligned in the same manner of beauty as Svetlana and Loraine. They all look so similar that it's painful. Well, they each have their own strikingly unique features, but they all look like models. God, it's so humbling being in their presence.

"I like her," Justine says with a smile on her lips, tilting down her sunglasses to get a better look at me. I look at her large brown eyes and see something terribly close to lust in them. I want out of this house. I can't stand it anymore. "Robby will love her," she says to Remi with a smile.

"You're right," he says, looking me over with that same hungry look on his face that Justine has. "Where you taking her, Bartrand?" he asks my golem.

"None of your business," Bartrand growls under his breath.

"What's your name, love?" Remi asks me and I look at Bartrand, feeling the tension dripping out of the air. Maybe that's something I can use to my advantage.

"Claire," I tell him, walking toward Bartrand's car.

"Claire, what a lovely name," Justine says, draping her arm over Remi's shoulder in a sign of ownership. She doesn't seem threatened by me, but clearly she has a thing for Remi. I'm trying to take in everything I can from these people that I can use against them. "Looks like you'll fit in just fine. Rufus only likes the pretty ones, has all of the ugly ones thrown away."

"And he only likes the strongest fighters," Justine continues, with a wide smile, her eyes turning to her beloved Remi. I watch her as she strokes his cheek. "See you soon, Claire. Don't be a stranger."

I nod as Bartrand opens the door for me, offering me a seat in the back. There's already a driver in the car, as if he was waiting for us the entire time. Dropping into the seat, Bartrand closes the door behind me, taking the passenger's seat up front. I feel the car start, but it's barely audible. This car probably costs more than I've made in my entire life. As the car starts to pull away, I look back at the house, wondering if I'm ever going to be able to escape this place.

Yes, I think I will be able to. Rufus has to have a weakness. There's nothing here for me that's worth sticking around for.

The world passes me as we pull out of the long, forested driveway and return to the main artery toward the city. I look at the road in a new light, wondering when I'm ever going to see this street the same way again. I'm going to have to suffer this estate and mansion for a while, that I'm certain of. I have no doubt that they're going to try and keep me for a very long time. But I won't give in, that much I swear.

After an hour, we make it back to my apartment, a strange, ghostly place now. Bartrand follows me to the door as I unlock it and slowly enter. The halls are empty and cold, forgotten, relegating themselves to a former life and accepting that fate. I look around at the pictures on the wall and see their faces as if they are ghosts in a cemetery. There's a moment where I think that I could just make a run for it, lock myself in the bathroom and try to squeeze out the window, but what good would that do?
What good would trying to run do for me, with Bartrand right on the other side of the door? No, I need to buy my time, be smart about everything. Going insane right now wouldn't do me any good.

"Need any help?" Bartrand asks me, uncharacteristically polite. I'm not going to buy it. Bartrand is not a friend. He's an enemy. I won't make the mistake of trusting him.

"I'm fine," I tell him bluntly. He looks at me with his cold, unforgotten eyes. They're as cold as ice.

"You shouldn't be so angry," he tells me. "There are worse fates than being pampered and cared for."

"You expect me to like being a sex slave for Rufus?" I snap at him angrily. "Just to be some sort of baby maker for a bunch of freaks?"

"You're being overly dramatic," Bartrand says coldly. "You're not marrying him, you're not tied down by him. Resisting is pointless."

"I could run," I tell him coldly. "You have no idea what I'm capable of."

"I know what you don't know," he says bluntly. "You have no idea what you're up against. You don't know that our lives work as reverse dog years. For every one year that you age, it takes us seven years. Our kind lives for centuries. We will never stop hunting you, and Rufus's pack is one of the best. It's the reason I joined up with him."

"What do you mean? Aren't you all related?" I ask him, lifting an eyebrow.

"No," he answers coldly. "Remi, Roman, and Robert are all Rufus's brothers. Their father was the original patriarch of the Clan of the Wolf, until Rufus killed him in a civil war. I came from the Clan of the Bear. I joined Rufus when he killed his father. Right now, he has the largest standing army of shifters on the East Coast."

"There are others like you?" I grab a bag out of the closet and start stuffing it with clothes and mementos. "What do they think about Rufus having me?"

"They don't know," Bartrand says coldly. "The Clan of the Ram and the Clan of the Bear have been circling for years, looking for a weakness in Rufus's estate. You better pray that they don't find out about you, or there's going to be a war to try and claim you. Last clan to try and take on Rufus was nearly annihilated. If you don't cooperate, Claire, a lot of blood is going to be on your hands."

I look at him, liking the sound of that. These things aren't supposed to be alive. So why should I worry about their survival?

*

The estate never changes. I've come to that conclusion, finally, and I don't think that there's anything about this place that changes, even the people. I look at the driver and Bartrand on the way back, studying them. There's nothing about them that seems friendly or amicable. But then again, that might just be because of Bartrand. If he's not from the Clan of the Wolf, then maybe they treat him as an outsider for a reason.

There might be something to exploit there, but I don't want to be too reckless about this. I know that plotting their downfall is going to be crucial to surviving, but I need to be smart about how I do it.

Infighting should be a last resort, not something that I start with. If anything, I should consider the prospect of a war, but how am I supposed to do any of this? If my survival is so important, then they won't risk losing me. I know that much. They'll stop at nothing to make sure that I stay in their hands, even if that means fighting a war.

"You should consider warming up to Rufus," Bartrand tells me calmly, watching the gates opening. I take note of the iron wolf head on the center of each gate, ornate and opulent. Everything about this place is designed to remind people of who owns it. It is a fortress for the Clan of the Wolf, but does that mean that it should be noticeable?

I mean, does the government know about these people? Do they all go berserk when the moon is full? Should I be worried about stuff like that? Suddenly, I remember that Bartrand is talking to me. "He can make your life a lot easier, or more difficult if you don't get on board."

"I'm nobody's sex toy," I tell him sternly.

"You're not a sex toy." Bartrand shakes his head at me. "You're the most prized possession that he owns."

"So, I'm his property," I snap at him.

"If you have to be property, why not be treasure?" Bartrand shrugs, like that's supposed to make me feel better. I shake my head, refusing to give him the satisfaction. I'm not interested in being the property of anyone. I look out the window at the enormous mansion. What does Roman think of all of this? Is he fine with me being his father's plaything? Did he have no feelings for me? Were they all in my head?

When the car stops, Bartrand steps out and opens the door for me, like he's being a gentlemen, or my manservant. I don't know which is more annoying. Everything about this place is a façade, a lie to keep people from suspecting the truth about them. I don't want any part of it, yet, here I am. Make the most of it, Claire, I tell myself over and over.

I have to keep strong. I have to keep my eyes open to everything. Every last detail will come in handy in the future. I'm going to need it to keep alive.

I figure that if everything goes fine and I somehow manage to survive having this baby and I end up having to be Rufus's baby maker, then I'm going to continue getting pregnant every time I pop out one of his brats. That can only happen for so long until I either die from it, or I'm no longer able to have children, and if Bartrand is right, they won't have aged more than a few years in that amount of time.

They'll slit my throat and leave me for dead until they find another. I doubt they're going to cut me a check for all my hard work giving birth to their next generation before they send me out and on my way. No, there's no hope of that. I have to make the most of this. I have to find some way of getting through this with some sort of dignity and advantage.

"I'll have a servant bring your things to your room," Bartrand assures me with his cold, harsh eyes on me at all times. I look into them, feeling as cold as they look. There's something potent in those eyes. I want to escape that gaze. I want to be free of his eyes, but I refuse to show him that. I give him an understanding nod before walking past him, hugging myself as I approach the house. Inside, I can hear music softly drifting out, washing over me. It's something soft and melodious, classical from what I can tell.

Inside, the elegance of everything remains the same, as timeless as everything else. I don't know what to do here. Am I really supposed to just stick around and wait for this baby to be ready to be born? I feel nauseous and tired already, but that should still be a few weeks off. I literally got pregnant last night. How could all of this be happening so sudden? Do shifters have normal pregnancies? What am I asking myself? Is any of this inherently normal or am I just a completely crazy person now?

"You're back?" Loraine asks me, her dark, jet black hair pinned up in a bun. She looks like she's been hand tailored by some designer's wet dream. Everything about her screams fashion and excess. I want to know their history—the story behind all of this. But most of all, I want to know what it means to be a shifter and why I should care about my future child being one.

"Good, that didn't take long at all," she says with a smile. "Rufus is busy upstairs with Justine and Nadine."

"Who is Nadine?" I ask her, stopping and watching as a pair of servants rush out to the car to gather my things.

"She's Justine's twin," Loraine says with a shrug. "They're not identical, unfortunately. That would have been greatly amusing, but nonetheless, Rufus likes to address them together."

"Address them?" I cringe, too afraid to ask, but I can't help myself.

"Fuck them," Loraine says bluntly.

I feel like she just slapped me across the face with a wet fish. I want to smile and laugh at the lunacy of it all, but her face is so very cold and pleasant that it would feel too insulting to do so to her. "But aren't you his wife?" I ask her, trying to wrap my head around all of it.

"No," Loraine shakes her head. "Marriage is a religious institution created by mortal man to give their lives another aspect of meaning. So many mortals seek meaning and purpose in love, a mundane, futile, and treacherous path to search for purpose, I assure you.

"But we shifters see ourselves as a bit more enlightened. Sex is for two things, pleasure and reproduction. Intimacy is something that people put inside of sex to make it more complicated than it has to be. Rufus is patriarch of this clan and is entitled to the bodies of any of the women belonging in our clan. He is our alpha.

"As the matriarch, I oversee the governing of the estate and have the second most powerful voice in the clan meetings. It's the highest a woman could hope to rise in a clan and the title is mine. Who Rufus fucks is none of my concern, unless it's me, and when he wants to fuck me, he can do so however and whenever he sees fit."

"That's very bizarre." I shake my head at all of it. "But Remi and Justine seemed like they were a couple."

"Some of the younger shifters spend far too much time among the mortals of this world." Loraine shrugs, giving me a sidelong glance "They see themselves as a coupling, yes, but it means nothing. Remi cannot stake claim to Justine and she cannot save herself for Remi. She can make a vow to only have sex with Rufus and Remi, but that's it. She must always be willing to submit to Rufus's desires and those desires are great indeed."

"It seems barbaric," I say to her.

"Perhaps, but a bit of hedonism is entitled to the leader of our clan," Loraine says to me, watching the servants bringing in my belongings. "Think of him as our King and God. But more importantly, think of me as your Queen and Jesus."

I nod to her, understanding exactly what she's trying to convey to me. "You just seem so young to be a matriarch," I tell her with a smile.

"Are you trying to flatter me?" Loraine grins, delighted by the comment. "It's doing wonders for you, I assure you. Yes, I am very young to be a matriarch. Penelope, Rufus's old matriarch was my mentor. I had her deposed when I was thirteen. I made Rufus have sex only with me for a whole mortal year as proof of my dominance."

"Thirteen human years? Or shifter years?" I ask her.

"Shifter years, you pervert," Loraine declares, shocked at the notion. I don't feel bad at all. How am I supposed to keep up with any of this? One moment, she's talking about how simple-minded marriage is and how hedonism is a privilege for the patriarch. I just assumed they were completely without any moral standards.

"I think we're going to be very good friends," she says to me with a big smile on her face as she offers her arm for me to take, a gesture that I recognize from Roman. Are they all so princely and polite at first? When do the claws come out? I'm waiting for that.

"Come, we need to make sure that you're fit and healthy and that our little treasure inside of you is coming along fine. Thank the Wolf you're beautiful and strong. The last vessel we found was fat and hideous. It'll be nice to see what handsome babies come from all of this."

I follow her along the corridors of the enormous estate, looking at all of the closed doors. I find it so strange that there are this many doors that are completely locked and closed. Don't people usually keep doors open to help make things feel open and airy for the people inside the house? The dance hall from the party is familiar, but it's so empty now that it seems ghostly and haunting to me as we stroll around the perimeter of it.

"Doctor Mason is a privy to our estate only because he has no true power anymore," Loraine tells me as we walk. I catch that she smells amazing; some kind of perfume no doubt. I don't know what it is that they're looking for exactly with a special doctor, but I'm glad that I won't have to deal with all of this in a medieval environment.

"There's a long history of violence and bloodshed that you're not aware of, but know that the Clan of the Wolf has enemies and that Rufus does not tolerate his enemies. The Clan of the Raven was one of his enemies and Doctor Mason Rothage was one of the few spared after our little war. He lingers as a sort of trophy to our victory, reminding the other clans not to bother trying to fight us."

"Impressive," I tell her, not sure if I mean it or not. From what I can tell, most of this past history seems completely violent and dangerous. I hope they're proud of it.

"Is he specialized in this sort of thing?" I ask her. "You know, an OB/GYN?"

"Doctor Mason has dedicated his life to the care of shifters," Loraine tells me. "He'll know about your lower anatomy as well. Don't worry about that."

When Loraine stops walking, I realize that we've come to the door that I'm supposed to go into calmly and collectively, like this is completely normal and fine.

She turns and looks at me, planting her hand on the door to stop me for a moment. "One thing you should know, Claire," Loraine says to me with a smile on her sweet, plump lips. "You give off a pheromone that will be hard to resist for many shifters. It's nearly irresistible; so don't hold it against the males of our species for any... inappropriate behavior that they might exhibit. I assure you that they're not trying to rape or molest you. It's easier if you just learn to be strong and enjoy it."

I look at her, utterly disbelieving what I'm hearing. She expects me to feel fine about being handled like some sort of sexpot by the men of every shifter clan around. No thank you. I watch as she opens the door, slowly showing me what looks like a state of the art medical facility completely fitted for a single room. Inside of it is a man with short honey blond hair that's extremely curly. He lifts his glasses, talking to one of the servants in a stern, yet collegiate voice, the kind of voice that you'd expect from a doctor.

"Where is the patient? I'm tired of playing these games," Mason says, before turning and getting a look at me. He stops his complaining and immediately adjusts his thick black frames and blinks several times. "By the Raven," he says with a deep sigh. "Loraine, what have you done?"

"Settle down, Mason," Loraine says, taking a seat next to the table that I'm apparently supposed to take a seat on. "Roman's already done what you're thinking about doing to her."

"A vessel?" Mason says with a deep, bewildered sound in his voice. "My word, Loraine. Do you have any idea what this means?" Suddenly, he snaps out of it and shakes his head before looking at Loraine sternly, completely confused by something. "Roman? You're telling me that Rufus gave Roman the first shot at impregnating the vessel?"

"It wasn't on purpose," Loraine tells him. "All the men in this family have been hunting for a vessel ever since the last one died on us. Roman just happened to be the lucky one to get there first."

"I bet Rufus is pissed," Mason says before gesturing to the table. "Here, come take a seat, miss...?"

"Claire," I tell him, obliged to take a seat next to him on the table. Why bother putting up a fight when I'm stuck here for the moment? Besides, I want to know what's going on inside of my body, and maybe Mason will be able to shed some light on what I should expect in the future of all of this.

As I sit down, I notice that the man is practically salivating over my presence. I wonder if Bartrand felt the same way and just had a better way of controlling it, unlike Mason. He gently puts his hand on my knee and smiles at me.

"Everything's going to be all right, Claire," he says softly, his hand gently resting on my knee. I can't shake it. I hate the feeling of it. "I'm going to take some tests and see how far along you are."

"Do you have a lot of experience with this sort of thing?" I ask him, moving my knee so he knows that I'm not comfortable with him touching me. He immediately removes his hand.

"Vessel pregnancies?" Mason asks me with a grin. "Yes. Lucky for you, I'm one of the few who does. There aren't many shifters out there that care about the health and safety of vessels. To them, you're pretty much just a baby factory."

Loraine clears her throat and my suspicious are confirmed. Mason looks at her and suddenly goes pale. "Shouldn't we get to work, doctor?" Loraine says modestly. I smile at her and Mason begins his work.

I endure him touching me and prodding me. While he works he tells me little bits of information that I've already known for a very long time. Babies have never been a mystery to me. I listen to him tell me all sorts of information that doesn't add up.

As he's telling me the things he's noticing, I know that this isn't possible. I'm nearly two months along and I could only have gotten pregnant last night. Why is all of this happening so quickly? Is there some sort of secret to all of it that I'm not understanding? I look at

Mason as he's talking, feeling his hands on my vagina as he works, feeling suddenly more than willing to let him keep touching me.

It disgusts me, but maybe deep down inside something Loraine said might have resonated with me. Just enjoy it, I tell myself as his fingers linger just a little too long on me.

"Loraine, this is incredible," Mason says, slowly pulling his fingers out from under the gown he's made me change into. "You have to tell the other clans. They have to know about this."

"They don't need to know a thing," Rufus's voice cuts through the room like a razor and I turn my head sharply to look at him. He's wearing a bathrobe of red velvet, ornately decorated with stitched wolves. Mason looks at him nervously as Rufus approaches me. "Claire is a prize that only the Clan of the Wolf will have the honor of sharing."

"But you must look at the larger picture," Mason declares. "Our entire species' survival depends upon having a healthy, strong vessel. War and feuds have plagued our clans to the brink of extinction."

"You're telling me to share my advantage with my enemy?" Rufus laughs cruelly. "Mason, you of all people should know that I'm not the merciful type."

Mason shakes his head. "If they find out that you're in possession of a vessel, then they'll unite against the Clan of the Wolf. There will be a new war for her."

"So be it." Rufus shrugs. "All I have to do is call Robert for aid and he'll assemble an army twice as large as anything the other clans can muster." Rufus looks at me, lifting his hand and gently stroking my cheek with his ringed fingers. His fingers are soft, disgusting. I want to vomit at the feeling of them on my skin.

"I think we're done here, Doctor," Rufus says bluntly. "Claire, you can dress and Bartrand will show you to your chambers. Loraine, come with me. We have business to discuss. Doctor, you can see yourself out. Remember, tell anyone and your life is forfeit."

"Yes, Rufus," Mason nods as they leave the room.

I watch them go and gather up my clothes, looking at Mason as he works silently, brooding over his briefcase. Quietly dressing, I watch as Mason steals glimpses of me out of the corner of his eye. I feel nervous, but I have nothing to lose.

"You should tell them," I say to him softly, worried that the room might be bugged.

"What?" Mason turns and looks at me, suspicious.

"Tell the other clans." I spell it out for him. "If I'm as valuable as you say I am, then you can't leave my fate in Rufus's hands. The man's a lunatic."

"Rufus is an extremely powerful man," says Mason, shaking his head. "Crossing him is suicide."

"So you'd just give him more power?" I egg him on. "Why, are you his pawn? He destroyed your clan. Besides, isn't the survival of the species more important than Rufus's happiness?"

CHAPTER SIX

I don't know what a shifter war looks like, but I'm fairly certain that I've just started one as I leave the examination room. Something inside of me feels sick and excited by the thoughts I've given Mason. Closing the door behind me as I finish buttoning my blouse, I realize that Bartrand is standing right in front of me, watching me. I look up at him, feeling violated by the look in his eyes. It's not lust or arousal, but simple assessment of what he's looking at, like I'm livestock that he's judging. It's almost insulting after seeing what I did to Mason.

"Is there something you needed?" I ask him rudely, tired of all of his head games.

"You're a fool," Bartrand tells me in his usual blunt tone. "Mason is a spineless coward. If you hope that he is your way out of this life, then you're sadly mistaken. If anything, Mason will use you as leverage to gain favor with another clan, to shift the tide of power. In the end, you will remain a slave to whoever owns you. Would you just trade one master for another?"

"I don't know what you're talking about." I shrug at him.

"Let me tell you what I'm talking about." Bartrand steps forward angrily, but there's a sort of reserved appropriateness to him that makes me feel slightly safe in his presence. "If Mason does what you've suggested to him, then war will ravage the Shifter world and you will be at the heart of it. Unless Rufus's enemies slay him immediately, he will kill you long before he ever lets you go with them. He is a stubborn, reckless man. In the end, you're not going to win, no matter what."

"I have to do something," I tell him bitterly. "You're no help to me and if I don't do something, then I'm nothing more than a slave for the rest of my life, forced to have monster babies until I'm no more use to Rufus."

"Bide your time," Bartrand says to me coldly. "There are more vessels out there. Wait until we find another one and perhaps he will let you go."

"Does he seem like the kind of man who lets others play with his things?" I ask him rationally. I know men like Rufus. They're just like Jake. How am I supposed to trust any of them? The best way to deal with men like Jake and Rufus is to beat them at their own games.
    "Perhaps not," Bartrand says. "But be careful. I know what it's like to be an outsider in this house."

I look at him, almost feeling like I've found an ally here, but that's not something I plan on dealing with right now. Bartrand is Rufus's man, whether I want to believe that or not. I'm not going to delude myself with ideas that he's on my side. He's a mercenary; loyal to survival and whatever he wants, not to anyone else. I can't expect him to be an ally, not now, not ever.

Bartrand takes me to the second floor of the estate's mansion where he guides me down the hallway to a room that's specifically for me. I don't think that there's anything about this room that looks like me, other than the two bags on the bed and the suitcase at the foot of it. It's too rich, too wealthy, not something that I'm looking forward to living in for the rest of my life. I take a deep breath and decide that it's time to take a break. I look at Bartrand who is still standing by the door, silently watching me survey the room.

"What should I do if I'm hungry?" I ask him.

"There's a bell by your bed," Bartrand says, gesturing to the blue button on the black stand. I look at the glowing blue button and feel like I'm living in some sort of fantasy. There's no way that I'm actually in a mansion with servants here to wait on me. I shake my head at the insanity of it all, but Bartrand seems completely lost to why I'm bewildered by all of this. "Is there a problem?" he asks.

I glare at him.

He shrugs, as if understanding why I'm not his biggest fan right now. "Should Rufus need you at any point, I'll be sent to find you. Try not to do anything suicidal in the meantime."

"I'll try not to," I say to him.

* * *

He wasn't kidding when he said that all I had to do was hit the little, glowing blue button. There's something about the way they come in and deliver whatever I ask for and immediately scurry away that unnerves me. I watch as they refuse to speak to me other than confirming what I'm asking of them or explaining to them what I want. When they look at me, the expression in their eyes is something unnaturally fearful. I take advantage of everything they give me, though.

When a knock comes at my door, it's been days since I've heard from anyone.

I spent most of my time watching television and trying to figure out how large this place is. I take nightly walks around the grounds, looking at all of the closed doors. Sometimes I run into people. If they're part of the known shifters that I've met, they're usually pleasant. But the staff is terrified of me, keeping their distance always. From what I can tell, I'm the closest thing to a demon they know, which is strange to me.

But when I look up at the door, I feel completely caught off guard.

Throwing off the blankets of my bed, I make my way toward the door, gently opening it and seeing that Bartrand is on the other side. He looks at me, at a loss for why I'm not opening the door more.

"Can I help you?" I ask him, unwilling to open the door any more for him.

"What are you wearing?" he asks me coldly.

"None of your business." I feel violated by him asking me that.

"Put on something sexy," he tells me callously, disinterested in my feeling violated or molested. "Rufus has asked for you to dine with him."

"I just ate," I tell him.

"Do you think Rufus cares about that?" Bartrand says. "You have ten minutes."

For the first five minutes, I stand with my back to the wall listening to Bartrand as I wait, trying to figure out what I'm going to do. I don't want to have sex with Rufus, but I know that he's going to expect that much when I go up to meet him. That doesn't mean that I have to dress up like a Barbie for him to play with. In fact, I'm inclined to do the exact opposite of that. I don't want his hands on me and I don't want him to think that I'm in any way okay with this.

But then I remember what Bartrand warned me of, about Rufus not being the kind of man to play games with. Begrudgingly, I go to the walk in closet that I'd examined extensively in the past few days. Most of it is filled with lingerie for Rufus's pleasure.

I find something that is barely passable for me. I put on the pink lacy bra and panties that I find and immediately throw on a tank top and a pair of yoga pants, going for a casual lazy look rather than a sexy come have me you slutty wolfman look.

Right now, all I care about is getting this over with and moving on with my life. Taking a deep breath, I go to the door and open it gently, glaring at Bartrand who immediately looks me over and shakes his head.

"That's the best you can do?" Bartrand grunts.

"What's that supposed to mean?" I protest, completely offended by him.

Bartrand shakes his head. "You have a body that most women would be envious of," he says to me. "Why do you act like you don't enjoy your body? You've clearly put time into your appearance. So why not enjoy it?"

"Enjoy being some man's plaything?" I ask him.

"Fight as much as you want." Bartrand shrugs. "In the end, it's up to you."

"What?" I don't get that part. In fact, I really don't get that part. Why would I want him to have sex with me? Why would I do any of this willingly? "Come on," I grunt at him. "Let's get this over with."

Bartrand leads the way, like an executioner leading a prisoner to the electric chair. I'm not going to give him any satisfaction. I'm not going to look at him and I'm definitely not going to plead with him. He would probably enjoy that. Maybe that's what he gets off on, having helpless women begging him for help as they're dragged off to be fucked by some old guy who thinks he's a god for his weird family.

I glare at him as he walks in front of me, refusing to let him see me as we go. He can look at my ass that I worked so hard for as I walk through those doors. There's no way that I'm getting him off by begging.

He stops in front of a door and stretches out his arm, his hand gesturing toward the door in front of me. "He's waiting for you," he says to me coldly. But there's something more. I notice that he's not entirely sounding delighted, not that he's anything just barely above monotone when we talk, but right now, he almost seems slightly disappointed.

I look at him for a moment, wondering if it's at all possible that he might not be too excited that I'm going in there. I look at him with a glaring, scrutinizing gaze. Does Bartrand have a crush on me?

Rufus's room isn't like anything I would have expected. It's lavish in a sort of rustic, uniquely opulent way which caters entirely to a man who finds old wood regal and appealing. Everything is built with rich, deep woods that have been lacquered and varnished beautifully. There are tapestries on the walls, intricately stitched and sewn together in the symbols and crests of things that mean nothing to me. I can appreciate the look of it, but the actual purpose for everything in this room is lost on me. I notice the enormous fireplace and the mantle adorned with stuff that looks like relics for some ancient, lost world that they're all privy to, except for me.

Rufus, as usual, is among all of these old relics and statues, walking like a proud king from some old, forgotten kingdom that no one cares about anymore. He looks at me with his neatly trimmed, sable beard perfectly shaved to his pleasure. He's not fat or out of shape or even unattractive. Honestly, he has this appearance that makes him look like a very well-to-do professor who likes to sleep with his students.

His personality is what drives me away, not his looks. I cringe inside at the thought that I might actually find this man attractive. Why would I even want to sleep with him? He's practically forcing me to be his baby mama. He puts his ringed hand on the back of the chair he's standing by, and looks at me, studying me as if I'm some complex mystery for him to solve.

"It's good to see you, Claire," he says to me in a silver, velvety voice that is probably supposed to make me all wet inside but just makes me feel unclean. "I was hoping that we might be able to get to know one another better," he says, gesturing me to the couch in front of the fireplace.

I calmly make my way toward the couch, deciding that right now is not the time to fight him. Besides, I don't want to see what it looks like when Rufus gets angry.

"Would you like a drink?" Rufus asks me, making his way to the bar. As I sit down, I watch him, wondering what he's going to have in his glass. I think he's a scotch man. He has that look.

"Sure," I tell him, deciding that a little liquid courage might not be such a bad thing right now. "I'll have a martini."

"Dirty?" he asks me.

"Of course," I tell him, taking a seat on the couch and wondering just how long it's going to be until I'm free of this room. I cringe at the thought of the things I'm going to have to do to escape this place.

He finishes making the drinks and makes his way to the couch, slowly sitting down next to me and handing me mine. I take it and down it almost immediately. I feel the familiar burn and enjoy the flavor while I can. It'll take a second for me to actually feel the effects, so hopefully I'll have some time until then.

"You must think that I'm something terrible," Rufus says to me with a smile on his lips. Clearly, he doesn't care what I think about him. "If you must know, I am a very kind and generous man, Claire," he tells me. "I'm a tender and practiced lover."

Practiced? Is that supposed to comfort me? The fact that he's a man whore has no standing on how I feel about him. In fact, I'm inclined to think less of him now. But, I think I understand what he's trying to say. I suppose if I have to have sex with a man, it might as well be slightly enjoyable. I place the martini glass on the coffee table and look at Rufus. I can feel the effects. It's nice. It's comforting. Maybe I'll be able to endure this.

"How many vessels have you had before?" I ask him, genuinely curious.

"I met a vessel once," he tells me, taking a drink from whatever it is he's put in his glass. "It was back when I was younger, too young to be patriarch. She was older, sickly and only gave birth to two before she died. We've never found one as young as you or as… attractive. It's an honor, truly."

"Lucky for me," I say.

"Well, I hope you know that I intend to take very good care of you," he tells me, gently putting a hand on my knee. Yep, there it is. I wish I had another drink, but I'm grateful for what I have. I'll take whatever I can get right now. His hand finds the fold in my house robe and pulls it open, revealing my yoga pants. He smiles at the sight of it, his hand moving to the inside of my thigh. "You're such a splendid woman, Claire. I'm a very lucky man to have a vessel who is so desirable."

I feel his hand moving up the inside of my thigh and I try to relax, feeling the side of his fingers gently brushing over my panties. His hand finds my hips and busy fingers maneuver around the hem of my tank, touching my bare skin underneath. His fingertips are warm, inviting. When he touches me, it tingles. I let his fingers explore me, pushing up, running over my abs and racing up to the bottom of my bra. As he cups my breasts, I lean back on the couch, feeling his eyes on my neck and face. He's studying me, taking every in little detail.

"Would you like me to continue?" he asks, as if I have much of a choice. I feel warm inside, brave and dangerous. I'm only going to be stuck here, every night, coming back to this room unless I tell him yes and when I do, hopefully it'll stop. But until then, he'll keep asking me. I look at him, not giving him any words, just shrugging off my house robe. When he sees this, the smile on his face could stretch a mile.

He leans in and kisses my neck, continuing to feel my breast with his hand and wrapping his arm around my waist with the other, drawing me closer to him. I feel the warmth of his body against mine, wishing that I wasn't wearing so much clothing. I reach down and grab the bottom of my tank top, pulling it off as I move away from him. Maybe it's the hormones, but I want this. He looks at me in just my bra as I discard my tank and I feel wild, desired, something I've never felt before.

Before I can say a word to him, he pounces on me, pushing me back onto the couch and kissing my chest and my stomach, ravenously racing his hands all around my body, feeling me as he pushes down my yoga pants.

I lean back, feeling the tingling, electric sensation with every kiss and every touch. I want him to do whatever he likes. I want him to have what he wants. I reach behind my back, unhooking my bra as he pulls my pants down. I kick them off as my bra falls limply to the ground.

"You are a remarkable vessel," he says breathlessly, reaching forward and grabbing my breasts with the intensity and ferocity of a man possessed by lust. My nipples are puffy and alert, begging for his lips and he happily obliges them. He squeezes one with his fingers and wraps his lips around the second, licking and sucking on them, shooting bolts of euphoria through me, shredding my inhibitions. I reach out and feel under his own silk robe, hunting for his blazing cock. I find it, rubbing it as his hips begin to pump and sway.

I have this man by the pinky and he's my slave. I could demand anything from him and I know that he would give it to me. I smile as his fingers brush over the lips of my vagina, making me squirm with delight.

"Yes," I tell him. "Do it."

"You're sure about this?" he asks me, raising an eyebrow.

"Yes," I whisper to him.

*

On the way back to the room, Bartrand is as silent as a grave. I feel incredible, like I've just had the greatest sex of my life. I don't know if that's true or if there was something a little extra in that cocktail that Rufus gave me, but no matter what it is, I feel like I'm on cloud nine. I'm glad that I said yes to him. I glad that I had the courage to get it over with. Besides, in the end, I'm actually quite pleased with myself. I learned a lot and, more importantly, I'm still learning.

I watch Bartrand walking ahead of me, refusing to look at me. When we finally make it back to the room that's been designated as mine, he turns and looks at me with his cold, merciless eyes.

"You enjoyed yourself?" he asks me, but it sounds like an accusation. I feel sick to my stomach looking at him. I've thrown up more in the past few days than I've ever done, and yet, this makes me feel sick. This makes me feel repugnant. How could he be so smug, so self-righteous right now? He's done nothing to help me and I'm not interested with him being torn up about this. But it's nice to know that he has these feelings. It's nice to know that Bartrand has a weakness.

"Maybe I'm learning to enjoy it," I tell him cruelly. He looks at me with his cold eyes, opening the door for me. I walk in through the door, feeling like I need to take a shower. I don't bother saying farewell or good night to Bartrand. I think of him as little more than my goon who is supposed to escort me from place to place. I don't want to bother wasting time talking to him right now. He could have saved me from all of this, but he could really care less. It makes me furious. Now I'm some guy's concubine and he suddenly grows a heart. I don't even care at this point. I'm the only person I can count on.

I'm not going to try to find an ally here. My only hope now is Mason. A war might thin them out and I might be able to get rid of Rufus. I'm sure that whoever takes his place won't be a fraction of the trouble. Probably Roman or Remi will take power as the patriarch. I can deal with that much.

Walking into the bathroom, I take off my bathrobe and let it drop to the floor around my feet. I'm numb. There's nothing right now that I want more than to just get into the shower and pretend like all of this is a bad dream. I want to kill Roman for what he's done to my life.

I've never been conniving or cunning or devious, but now that's all I can hope to be if I want to survive. There's nothing here that can save me except for a dark heart.

Taking everything off, I look into the mirror, staring at myself. There's nothing sticking out to me right now except for how numb and emotionless I look. I feel like all of this is killing me. I have to get out of here. I can't just let Rufus keep having his way with me while men like Bartrand circle angrily.

Turning on the shower, I step inside, hoping that there's something on the horizon. Where is Roman? Why isn't he having more trouble with this than I am? Shouldn't he at least be trying to fight for me?

The night we spent together in his room and those dates we went on were incredible, and it couldn't have just been me feeling all of it. Maybe it was. Maybe I'm just a foolish, stupid little girl who got what she deserved for trying to live in a fantasy world. Life isn't like that. Life is real. Life is hard. Life is struggle and toil. I know that now. I'm willing to do what's necessary to get out of here.

As the water hits me, I feel relieved. I need to get out of here. Maybe one day, one day soon.

* * *

The mornings have become little more than routines of throwing up, lying in bed, and trying to find the will to survive. There's something about this place that makes me want to scream and run away. But right now, I don't think I have the strength to even make it out of the house. I'm tired of feeling so terrible. Every time I look in the mirror, I think that I can see a little more clearly that I'm pregnant, but I know that it's insane. Mason never had a chance to tell me what it was like for a vessel to carry a shifter baby, and maybe I don't want to know anymore. I think they grow fast. I think that I should be worried, but I refuse to give it any more thought. Right now, all I care about are the cravings and that it's so damn hot in here. I'm restless. I just want out of here.

Getting out of bed becomes harder and harder with each day that I spend in this room. There's something that makes it seem like it would all be better if I just stayed in this room, alone and away from everyone else. I don't know if this is some sort of plan of theirs' or if I'm just overly miserable, but I'm noticing how hard it is to get up.

But this morning, or afternoon, not sure which anymore, I'm done with lying around, being a victim. No, I'm going to get up and actually do something. I'm going to try and get more information. I need to be proactive about all of this. I'm not going to stand by and wait for them to take me back to Rufus for another sex night.

I make my way out of the room, watching for any signs of the maids and servants that litter this place. I can hear them walking outside and for every maid or servant that I see moving around, there are more of them lurking outside as gardeners and lawn care employees. I don't understand if they're all shifters or just a bunch of psychos going along with the plan.

No, I can't believe that they are all in on this. They have to be completely oblivious, or they wouldn't let them come and go as they do. I doubt that many of them even speak English. No, this whole place is completely insane. I bet it's meticulously cared for and screened by Bartrand or one of the others.

Out in the hallway, there's no one around and I slowly make my way down the hall, glancing at all of the locked doors, moving as silently as I can. I don't want to draw the attention of any of the shifters. The last thing I need is another creepy conversation about their convoluted past. Their history makes no sense to me. It's all violence and strange, clandestine clans. The more I hear about it, the less I actually understand. Their words are all wrong, strange and twisted.

When I make my way to the balcony, I stop and look out the window over the driveway, at the fountain, and everything going on below me. There's no way I could just steal a car and drive off. Every time I see a car show up, there's a driver involved with it. The only time there hadn't been a driver was when I saw Remi and Justine together.

At this point, I wonder if there's a way I could get to the garage without anyone noticing. Do they have a flock of drivers just walking around, waiting for their strange whims? No, they have to have access to cars. But, when I look out at the driveway, it's not empty as usual. There's a lot of commotion out there.

"See anything you like?" a voice asks. I'm startled by the suddenness of hearing it, but there's nothing about it that's too surprising. Someone always shows up behind me while I'm looking at something or trying to sneak around. I hate that about this place, but I've gotten used to it over the days.

I look over my shoulder at Remi who is approaching me, Justine clinging to his arm gently, lovingly. The look in her eyes as she glances at him looks like pure love and infatuation, something that is strangely endearing.

As I turn to look out the window, they come up next to me, staring out the glass and down at the driveway with me. The drivers standing next to the cars look oddly similar to bodyguards or goons that might be carrying weapons. I'm suddenly very concerned about what is happening. Is Rufus raising an army? Because, if he is, then I don't want to be here right now. Not right this minute, at least.

"I hear Rufus had a meeting with you," Justine says, looking at me with her big, wide eyes. She's so pretty that it's alarming. I don't feel like I fit in here, no matter how many times people keep telling me that I do.

"How was that?" she asks me. She reminds me so much of Loraine; they're all so polite, but strangely rude in the way that they pry.

"He fucked me," I tell her emotionlessly.

"And how was it?" Justine edges on. "I find that Rufus is a passionate lover, but he's very down to business. He doesn't take his time. It's all about him and what he enjoys in the moment. I suppose that it can be hot sometimes, but Remi is far more interested in everyone being happy."

"You're too polite." Remi grins at her. "Soon, he'll get bored with you, Claire. Don't worry. The man has an enormous sexual appetite. He needs diversity and variety. Some would call that a curse."

"A curse he deserves," Justine says bitingly. I find that odd. Something inside of me is piqued with curiosity by that statement. "Last time, he had me and my sister at the same time. I'm fine with threesomes, but not when it's my sister."

"You two don't like Rufus?" I ask them, lifting an eyebrow.

"Not particularly," Remi answers. "But liking him has very little to do with it. Our loyalty is to Rufus and it's unquestionable. He's just a bit old. He favors archaic tactics with the other clans that seem as applicable today as would Roman military styles in the Middle East. He needs to stop being so militant and realize that the survival of our species is in the balance, not the superiority of some supposed clan. There shouldn't be clans anymore, just shifters."

"I doubt that's a very popular stance," I say to him.

"Maybe, when you're a pig-headed idiot." Justine shrugs. She pushes away from the window and looks at me. "Come along, love. Rufus wants to show you off to his guests."

I really don't like the sound of that. Slowly, I make my way behind Justine and Remi as they whisper into each other's ears, casting glances over their shoulders at me as we walk. I find their sort of loving behavior endearing. They remind me of Chloe and Mark. I feel bad. I miss them. There's something heartbreaking about the life that I used to have. Everything seems so far away and forgotten. I wonder what they think happened to me. Were the police even called? Am I already a memory to them as well?

"What's going on?" I ask them as we approach the stairs going down to the next floor.

"You'll find out soon enough," Remi says to me. "They're in the dining room."

We're only a few feet away and when they approach the doors, a pair of servants open the doors for us. I'm surprised at the sight of so many people gathered around an enormous, sprawling table that's lined with ornate wooden chairs that look like they were stolen from some sort of palace. There are a lot of faces toward the far end that I don't recognize from the grounds before. Rufus and Loraine are seated at the head of the table nearest me.

"Ah, Claire," Rufus says over his shoulder. "So good of you to join us."

I look directly to where Roman is seated and I feel my blood boiling. He doesn't even bother looking at me. His stupid, handsome face looks just as perfect as the day I ran into him at Starbucks, but I can't help but want to beat it in. He barely glances at me for a second and then looks right back to his hands.

What a coward. Why does he think that he's going to get away with this? I'm going to have my revenge on him, I promise that much.

Rufus stands up and holds out his hands like he's presenting me like a prize one some sort of sick and twisted game show. "Claire, this is Vincent Coladio, patriarch of the Clan of the Bear and this is Lucius Pickerton of the Clan of the Ram. It seems that our beloved Mason has let it slip that you're in our company. So the patriarchs of our two beloved families have come to see for themselves it the word is true."

"You have a vessel?" A man that I'm assuming is Vincent shoots up from his seat and points at me. "Rufus, you think that you could find a vessel this young and that we wouldn't care? You dare to keep it a secret from the rest of us? You would put your own superiority above that of your people? Our entire species? How dare you!"

"How dare you, Vincent," Rufus snaps back at him. "I welcome you into my home, to show you the truth, and you accuse me of trying to sabotage our species' chance at survival? How dare you treat me as such?"

"Bullshit, Rufus," Lucius answers angrily. "If it weren't for Mason, you would have never told us that you had a vessel. You would raise your brood to strike us down the moment they were old enough and the numbers ensured your victory against a united army. Don't play coy with us. Do not insult us to our very faces."

"Fine, Lucius," Rufus says with a smirk on his lips. "What would you have of me? Do you want me to share my hard-fought and hard-sought-after prize? Sure, why don't we all have a turn with the vessel? Would that make all of you happy?"

My stomach sinks at the sound of that. It makes me want to scream, but there's nothing I can do or say that would make any difference in all of this. I'm just a pawn to Rufus. I'm just a pawn to all of these assholes. But as I look at Lucius and Vincent, I realize that what's happening here is exactly what I wanted. They're looking at me with envy and a sort of lust that is beyond the physical. They want me to be in their possession, not in Rufus's. I just hope that their envy is enough for them to try and take me by force.

"You think that this is a game?" Lucius says coldly, almost venomously. "Your power hungry warmongering is enough to get all of us killed. You know how rare a vessel is. We must utilize her so that all the bloodlines can continue. Leave the fighting and the killing for future generations. Right now, we need to ensure that those future generations have a chance."

"There will be a future generation," Rufus assures them. "Already, Claire is pregnant with the next generation of the Clan of the Wolf and then, when she has given birth to our heir, there will be another. She will continue to ensure the survival of our species for all time. Soon, there will only be the Clan of the Wolf, regardless of what any of you do to stop us.

"Because, though you think you stand a chance united, we all know that there's nothing you can do. Gather your armies and plot your schemes, there's nothing you can do here. You are at my mercy. Accept it, and we might be able to work something out."

"Go to hell, Rufus," Lucius says, rising. His bodyguards rise with him and I can tell that they're not happy one bit. I hope that anger I see inside of them is enough to spark something more. I feel like Rufus has done enough right now that I won't have to fuel the flames much more. All I need is these other clans to have a little fight in them. "You should reconsider this stance you've chosen."

"Perhaps it is you who should reconsider, Lucius," Rufus says to him as Vincent and Lucius both leave the room, glaring at Rufus as they go. I watch as Lucius gives Bartrand an especially cold glare. It's something that has meaning to it and I try to hold on to that. I should ask him about it later. When they've gone, I can feel the electric tension in the room. The doors close behind them and everyone looks to Rufus, waiting for him to say something.

I watch him with worried eyes. There's something that sticks out to me right now. I have no idea where Mason is. Did I just get him killed? Rufus rises from the table. "Call the others, Roman," he says coldly. "Bartrand, Remi, I want security beefed up. Doctor Mason performed admirably." He turns and looks at me. "You played your part remarkably well, my dear. Your pleading for his help definitely sold him on it. Well done."

I feel a cold, sinking feeling in the pit of my stomach. This is exactly what he wanted. I've just played into Rufus's plan.

CHAPTER SEVEN

"There's something I want to show you," Rufus says to me in a cold, almost delighted tone. The sinister look in his eye tells me that this isn't something that I want to hear. I watch as a platinum blonde enters, hardly wearing any clothing at all. She looks at me with a cold, disinterested gaze that almost seems slightly sinister. I realize that this is Nadine, Justine's twin sister.

As she walks by Rufus, I watch her put her arm on his shoulder and gently run her fingers across his arm. He looks at her with an approval in his perverted eyes. I watch her go as quietly as she came. That one's going to be trouble. Bartrand quietly comes up behind Rufus, replacing Nadine and looking at me with equally cold eyes. "I want to show you the fruits of your labor."

Everyone leaves the room and it's just the three of us left. Instinctively, I put my hand on my stomach, worried about what Rufus might do to me or to the baby. He's clearly not happy. I don't want to spark his anger. After seeing the meeting, I'm genuinely afraid of what Rufus might do right now. Rufus waves his hand for me to follow him.

Turning, I watch him head for the opposite side of the room, the opposite direction from where everyone else was going. I don't like this isolation. I look over my shoulder at Bartrand. I don't feel safe with him either. I can't trust him. He's loyal to Rufus and has no interest in me right now.

Rufus pushes open the door and I realize that I'm walking into the enormous sprawling kitchen, but there's no staff here. Everyone who makes the meals I order routinely has gone home or is in another part of the house. We're too alone. I hate this. Where is Roman? Where is everyone else? I'd take Remi and Justine right now if I could.

"I'm disappointed that you told Mason to alert the others," Rufus says to me as I realize that we're not entirely alone. There's someone in here with us. I look at the far end of the kitchen where a man is seated in a chair with glittering, silvery chains tied tightly around him. There's a bag over his head and I feel nauseous. I know already who it is that I'm looking at.

"But you have to understand that I'm a reasonable person. I know what power fear has, especially for someone who has just been introduced and imprisoned in this life. So I cannot blame you for your actions. But, in the end, Mason's actions were Mason's actions alone. I can't blame you for that."

Bartrand walks around the man who is chained to the chair and rips off the black sack over his head violently, mercilessly. I look at Mason who looks like someone beat him nearly to death. His eyes are swollen and bloody; streaks of crimson are running down his face. His lips are split and it looks like he's missing some teeth as well.

"But, Mason chose his path," Rufus says, walking to a drawer that's locked. He pulls out a key from his pocket and unlocks it, slowly sliding open the drawer and reaching inside. I can't tell what he's grabbing, but when his hand comes out, I see that he's holding something that's glittering and silver. After a second, I realize that it's a knife, a thick, large knife. It reminds me more of a machete than a knife. I feel nauseous again, like I'm going to throw up if he does something with it to Mason. I'm not built for that. I can't handle this. I need to stay away from the bloodshed.

"Isn't that right, Mason?" he says, approaching him with the silver machete.

"Please, Rufus," Mason pleads through broken teeth and torn lips. "Please, I had to tell the others. You can't do this. You have to share her, for the survival of our people."

"For the survival of my people, Mason," he snaps at him, pointing the machete at his face. "But I understand your concern. You've lost a lot of friends and family members over the years. You should be very proud to have endured for so long, but you have made a mistake. You have made an error in siding with my enemies, Mason. For that, you have to suffer the consequences."

"Please," Mason says, fumbling for the words in his broken mouth. "My people, the Clan of the Raven. You can't kill us all."

"I'm not going to kill you, Mason," Rufus says with poisonous words. I take a step back and feel Bartrand behind me. My God, I didn't even realize that he was behind me. He moves as silently as a cat or a ghost. I'm not sure which is more appropriate to him. "I'm going to teach you a lesson, that's all. There's no need to be afraid."

Somehow I don't believe him.

Before Mason can say anything to Rufus, I watch him lifting up the silver machete and bringing it down on Mason's hand that's chained to the armrest of the chair. With a single hack, I watch Rufus sever Mason's left hand, cutting it clean off with a single blow. As it falls to the ground, I watch the blood gushing out of his wound and feel suddenly faint. His hand is lying on the ground, fingers slightly clawed inward as he screams at the top of his lungs, screaming for mercy and in unimaginable pain. I know that I'm going to throw up. I can't handle this. I don't want to be part of any of this.

"Please." I feel myself whimpering the words. "Please, let me go," I

beg of him.

"You're part of us, Claire," he says to me in a cold, unforgiving tone. He wants me to understand this. I get that now, without question. I won't betray him again. Or at least, next time, I'm going to be a lot more careful about it. I won't play into his hand like this again. I have to be smarter than he is. I can't just be his pawn. I have to be his adversary. "The other clans will not be as kind to you as I am. You should be honored to be a part of our clan. I assure you."

Mason is whimpering, pleading with Rufus for mercy, for help. As I feel Bartrand's hand on my shoulder, I know that I'm in way over my head. God, I hope that the other clans are getting ready for war. I hope that they come and storm this place. They need to do it soon, or I won't be able to run when they get here.

* * *

I flush the toilet, washing away the puke. I don't think I'm going to be able to do this. I've never once thought that I would see something like that. Who could ever imagine seeing something like that, something so horrible? I take a moment to look at myself in the mirror, trying to understand what it is that I've done. Mason is missing a hand now because I foolishly tried to get him to help me. How could I have done this? How could I have been so stupid? There's nothing here that can help me. I'm on my own. I can't put other people at risk. Escape is my only option now. I know that.

Looking in the mirror, I see a frightened girl who is too scared to do what's necessary. I shouldn't be afraid of bloodshed. Running away cowardly is a fool's strategy. If I'm going to get out of this, then I'm going to have to get my hands dirty. There's nothing clean about what needs to be done. I have to get out of here by any means necessary, so what am I thinking? Why am I thinking that I'm not going to be able to get my hands dirty? Escaping is not going to be an option, not without Rufus and the others dead. I take a deep breath. I can do this. I have to be able to do this. I have to be strong.

"You can do this, Claire," I tell myself. There's a knock on the door. Bartrand is waiting for me. He's lurking just beyond the door and no doubt listening to everything that's happening inside. I look at the door and glare at it. There's nothing in here that concerns him. Why can't he just leave me alone for a second? I want to punch him in the face.

I turn toward the door and open it, looking at Bartrand who is staring at me blandly. He knows what I've been doing in there, but he doesn't even bother acknowledging it. He stares off into the distance like the golem he is for me. I hate the sight of him. He's the bars of my prison and I want to shy away from him.

As he walks toward my room, I follow him silently. This whole place is scarier now, darker and shadowy. It's like I'm living in hell and Bartrand is my own personal demon to haunt me and guide me through it.

Back in my room, I listen as he closes the door behind me, still hearing Mason's screams in the back of my mind. I can't think of him as a victim. No, he's one of the dozens of predators that are lurking around this house. He's a monster and a devil. As I look at the door, I wait for the sound of his footsteps to draw away from the room and I slowly sink onto the bed. There's something sad about this place now. There are stakes here and I know about them. I'm going to have to find a way out of this. I'm going to have to be smarter than I've been.

There's a soft knock at the door and I know that it's Bartrand, trying to say something or do something to change my opinion of him. I glare at the door. Too little, too late, big boy. I want to keep the door bolted, locking me away from all the horrors that are out there. In fact, I think I might. They can turn into savage wolves and blow down my door if they have to because that's what they're going to have to do if they want to get to me.

He knocks again and I feel like he's got a battering ram at the core of my sanity and is battering away at me. Grinding my teeth and clenching my fist, I feel like there are spider eggs inside of my mind, hatching and scurrying every time he knocks.

"Go away," I snap at him, dropping down on the edge of my bed and trying to find the strength to keep on going. If I'd known that my actions would lead to me seeing a man's hand chopped off, I probably would have played things out differently.

"Claire, open the door," I hear a voice hissing to me. After a moment, I wrinkle my brow. I know that voice. It's only been a while, but I've almost completely forgotten about it. It's the voice of a ghost, someone who is long dead to me. Someone who has been relegated to hell with all the other demons of this house. I blink my eyes and stare over at the door. This isn't happening. This cannot be happening right now. I don't need this. I don't need him right now most of all.

"Go away, Roman," I growl at the door, truly willing to go throw it open and bash him in the face with one of the huge candle-holders on the mantle. Does he really think that there's any way in the world that I'd be willing to talk with him, let alone have a chat?

"Claire, come on," he hisses through the door again. "Open the door."

"No," I hiss back at him. "Go away."

"Damn it, Claire," he hisses at me with a sense of urgency in his voice. I glare at the door, wishing that I could strap dynamite to it and blow the thing off, incinerating Roman in the process. "You need to open the door before Bartrand comes back."

That piques my interest. There's a red light bursting in the back of my mind, shouting at me and telling me to be careful, that no one in this house is trustworthy. There's nothing I can do to know whether or not I can trust a word from any of them. Closing my eyes and taking a deep breath, I decide that it'll be worth knowing whatever game it is that Rufus is trying to play with me. Even if I don't bite, it'll be nice to know what piece of bait is lying on that sharp hook, but more importantly, I'll get a glimpse of the hook if I'm lucky.

Gripping the handle of the door, I slide the locks out of place and open up, looking at him on the other side. He's as handsome as he's always been, but there's something distinctly cruel and evil hanging about him, like the dark clouds of a storm hugging the horizon. God, I wanted so much from him. I wanted to believe in so much of him, a future and a world that wouldn't be so depressing and terrible, like this.

I don't want to be married to a man like him. I wanted to come home to him and lie in bed next to him, but that's not an option anymore. That's not a life I'll have, ever. He runs his hand through his hair and looks down the hall, making sure that there's no one watching us. He looks at me with his eyes burning right through me.

"I hear that Rufus took Mason's hand," Roman lets out a sigh as he says it. It's something that makes me feel nervous. I don't want to get in the middle of all of this, even though I'm involved already. I look at him, not sure what he wants me to say right now. Does he want me to confess to it? To step up and take responsibility? Like Rufus said, Mason made his choices. I didn't make them for him. "Are you okay?"

"What do you think?" I glare at him coldly. "How would you feel after watching a man chop off another man's hand?"

"I'd feel like shit," he says bluntly. Glancing down the hallway both ways again, making sure he's clear. "Do you need anything?"

"I'm fine," I growl at him. What does he want right now? I'm not going to forgive him. I'm not going to just step aside and let him have his way with me.

"Listen," he says, leaning in conspiratorially. This is it. This is the bait that's dangling on the line in front of me. I can see the hook. So this is how Rufus is going to try and get to me. He's going to try and use Roman? Is he a moron? Or is this some sort of dark insidious plan that he's hatching? I can play along, just for a little while longer, but I'm not doing a thing that Roman suggests.

I can see the strings reaching up into the ceiling and snaking all the way back to Rufus who is proudly sitting in his velvet chair making Roman dance. "I'm going to get you out of here," Roman says to me in a voice that's so hushed, I can barely hear it. "It wasn't you who got Mason into that mess. I'm the one that put the squeeze to him and got him to give up and go send word to the other clans."

"How'd you do that?" I ask him, not impressed at all. This is the best he can do? This is what brilliant scheme he's hatched? How is Roman supposed to buy back my trust by confessing to something I know he didn't do?

"I beat the hell out of him," Roman lies to me. "Listen, Claire. A war is coming. The other clans aren't going to hold for Rufus. They're going to want you for themselves. It's going to be unending bloodshed until there's no one left but you and the victor. I aim to make sure that Rufus takes a fall in the first battle."

"You'd betray your brother?" I lift an eyebrow, still not buying any of it.

"You bet I would," Roman says, leaning in. "Claire, Rufus was having me followed. Bartrand saw you and he tested your DNA from a cup you used at the club. He's suspected all along that I was hunting for a vessel and wanted to make sure that I was playing true to the clan. Unfortunately, he told Svetlana and they got to you first, before I could keep you secret—hidden from them."

How am I supposed to buy that? If he was really interested in my safety or security, then he would have acted sooner. He would have kept away from me or done whatever he had to do to protect me. He wouldn't have let Bartrand and Svetlana take me away if he really cared.

After all, what had he done since then to protect me? It had been weeks of me hiding in this room, trying to avoid them without a single peep from him. So where had he been all this time? I take a deep breath and shake my head at him. There's nothing that he can say that will ever make me want to trust him or believe him again.

"I don't believe you," I tell him bluntly.

"You don't have to," he tells me like some sort of romantic knight in shining armor. There's no way that he's going to save me from the harsh, cold truth about everything he is. I look at him feeling the cold fire hatred inside of me. "I'm going to show you that I'm telling the truth," Roman tells me coldly. "I'm going to do everything in my power to make sure that you're safe and that there's nothing that can harm you in the house."

112

Looking at him, I almost wish that I could believe him. If anything, this is Rufus's little trick to try and get me to safety while he massacres the rest of the clans in one desperate, violent fight. The reality is hard, permanent in my mind, something that makes me want to just melt into it. I take a moment to appreciate what Roman is trying to do.

"Roman," I tell him bluntly. "Go away."

*

I hear that they're keeping Mason in the cellar. I don't know what the point of that is, but it's what Loraine told me one day when she sat up with me on the bed while I ate ice cream and watched daytime television. I looked over at her with a confused expression on my face. She stared at me and told me that she knew that it was on my mind. It had to be, after all. I was responsible for a man losing his hand, so of course it was weighing on my mind. It always seems to come down to this. I take a moment to process what she was saying to me. It wasn't that a man lost his hand because of me, it was that Mason was being held in the cellar. Rufus was not letting Mason go. He was a prisoner here.

I looked at the door and then at Loraine who is wearing a silk bathrobe with lingerie underneath. She's waiting for Rufus to call her. I've come to learn that there's actually a schedule that Rufus follows. I look at the ice cream in my hands and I can't help but wonder what it is that Mason has been doing down there, chained to the wall, probably. Has he been thinking about all of the terrible things he wants to do to me the moment he gets free? Or is it Roman that he's looking to gut like a trout?

"Is there going to be a war?" I ask her, feeling that my most open enemy might be my only friend. I look at her with a brief hesitation, wondering if there's someone else that I should be talking to instead of her, but I doubt it. There's nothing here that is truly friendly. I'll take an honest captive to a lying monster.

"There better be," Loraine says with a smile, stabbing her spoon into her carton of Phish Food. "After all the fuss about you, then there better be at least a little bloodshed. More than a hand, at least. If you ask me, there are far too many progressives among the ranks of the shifters out there. We could use a good thinning of the herd."

"That's pretty brutal," I say to her bluntly. I'm not interested in making friends here. I've decided that playing it safe is the way to get killed. The only thing that I've got going for myself is the fact that I know that it's all a game and I'm not going to get caught off guard by it again.

"It's true," Loraine says with a heavy sigh, like she's got something caught in the back of her throat. "People like Remi and Justine think that it's something special to be normal, like humans, but it's not. What's special is that we can change our bodies and that we are superior.

"That's what is special, not living like cattle. I'm not interested in that. They shouldn't be interested in it either. Maybe a good bleeding and thinning will do the trick and put their heads on straight. A little tough love."

"Are you talking about killing them?" I say, almost aghast at what I'm hearing. Loyalty seems to be everything to these people and here's Loraine. She's completely Machiavellian right now and there's something about all of this that smells wrong to me.

"No," Loraine shakes her head. "But, if the fight gets brutal, then it'll be nice that I'm the Matriarch right about then. That's all I'm saying."

Unquestionable loyalty is one of the most precious things in this house and the fact that I can smell it all around Loraine and that it smells genuine is a scent that I've longed to breathe in. At the moment she looks away, I know that Loraine is not as loyal to Rufus as she would like us all to believe. I smile at that, taking another spoonful of Rocky Road and savoring it as I watch Fernando kissing Mrs. Cravett on the screen.

"About time they got together," Loraine says, jabbing a spoon at the screen with her lithe, perfect hand. I stare at the screen and smile. Yeah, it's a good feeling right now.

* * *

I don't know where I'm going, but the quiet of the house is soothing to me. My stomach looks like I'm four weeks pregnant and I'm nowhere near as close to that date as I look. Taking a moment, I look in the long mirror, feeling my stomach and wondering what's going to happen in the future; how much longer until I'm giving birth to whatever this abomination is.

There's something about it that terrifies me. The only person who might give me any kind of advice or indication of what's coming is locked up in a cellar right now. He's missing a hand. How is he going to help deliver this monster with only one hand? I'm screwed. There's no one here who can help me like Mason was supposed to help me.

I look down the long corridor of the mansion at all the locked doors. I don't know why I'm wandering around right now, but I know where I'm going. I know what's calling to me. I look down the hall at Rufus's room. The door is shut, black and glossy in the darkness of the night. The pale moonlight comes in through the windows that are always open, giving the whole world a brisk chill. I wonder if they keep the windows open even during the winter. That seems like a silly thing to think about right now, but it bothers me. There's something in the air tonight, biting at my mind, and calling to me for attention.

God, this is a stupid thing to do. I slowly walk toward the door, listening. I can hear the sounds from beyond the door, on the other side. The sounds are enough to make me wonder again what I'm doing out there. What do I expect to find beyond that door? There are no answers. There's no comfort for me in the arms of Rufus. I think about Roman and how he betrayed me—how I'm here because of him and his betrayal. It's enough to make me furious. The only thing I can hope for is to come to some sort of arrangement with Rufus. He's the man who holds my life in his hands.

I can hear him fucking someone on the other side. I don't know who it is, but from the sounds they're letting out, it must be one hell of a night. From what I figure, they always make it sound like that. I look at the door and reach out to feel the brass handle of the door. The cold texture under the skin of my palm tells me that I'm so close to Rufus. I should steer away. I should be smart about this. I take a deep breath. Let's do this.

Gripping the handle, I twist it and push open the door, surprised that there are no locks. Of course there are no locks on his door. This is Rufus's house. Everything that happens in this house is by the will and design of Rufus. No one would dare do a thing in this house without his approval. No one would dare open this door without his say so. As the door swings open, the warm glow of the fireplace sprawls across the room. I look directly toward where Nadine is straddling Rufus before the fire, her ivory skin cast in the warm glow of his fireplace.

Her head is thrown back, her pale, platinum hair swaying and flipping as she digs her fingers into his chest, grinding herself into his hips. As she moans and takes each thrust, I watch her breasts quake, her nipples pert and attentive. I watch her, reaching up and running a hand down her neck and over her breasts, giving her nipple a squeeze. It's fake. It's as fake as pornography.

But like so many men, Rufus is eating it up. His hands are clamped down on her hips, pulling her close to him. As she turns and looks down, her eyes settle on me, disapproving and disappointed that I'm here. While she looks at me, I notice that her hips keep pumping, grinding on Rufus as they keep fucking. Rufus turns his head, craning to get a look at me. When he sees me, a smile spreads across his face.

"Claire," he says, giving his sexpot another thrust. "A pleasure to see you. It's been a while."

"I was hoping we could talk," I say to him calmly.

"Is there no clock in your room?" Nadine asks me, bitingly. I look at her and try to bite my tongue. I'm surprised that I can. She hates me and unlike Loraine, she's completely loyal.

"Settle down, love," he says, patting her naked thigh. Apparently that's code for her to get off of him. She stands up, her lithe, nimble body looking like some sort of impure goddess. The sight of her naked before me is intimidating, especially with how bloated and huge I'm feeling right now. I look at her and want to punch her in her stupid face. Rufus wraps his waist with a sheet that they'd absconded from the bed. "What is it you need, my dear?"

"A private word," I tell him again. "That's all."

Rufus looks at Nadine, whose cold, icy eyes never leave me. I meet her gaze for a moment before turning to Rufus. He watches me with a cold, dark gaze that makes me curious as to what he's studying me for. I don't know what's happening right now, but he's definitely interested in me. He turns his head and puts a hand on Nadine's naked butt. "Give us the room," he says with a smile on his lips.

"Rufus," she turns and protests, looking at him with those cold,

azure eyes.

"Now!" He snaps at her angrily, glaring at her for daring to defy him. I feel the tension in the air, crackling like lightning all around me. She keeps his gaze for a moment before turning and walking away.

As she passes me, I swear that I can hear her growling at me. There's something feral in her throat that makes me feel unsafe. When the door latches behind her, I feel suddenly very alone with Rufus. As he looks at me, I feel like I'm the one naked before him. "Now, what was it you wanted to speak to me about?" Rufus says to me, inviting me over to the couch, closer to him.

Slowly, I walk toward the couch, nervous about what I'm going to say to him. I have no illusions about what's in my mind, what's lingering on my heart. I want to say the right thing because I want him to actually hear me. I want him to actually give me a chance to do what I want.

I'm tired of feeling like such a prisoner in my own skin. If I'm going to do this, then I need to have some hope. I need to have some guidelines in my life, from here on out. Taking another deep breath, I sit down across from him, looking at his unreadable face. He's watching me. He's eating up every last little motion and gesture that I make. He's trying to read me like a book. Good thing I've been practicing.

"I want out." I breathe out as I speak, slowly exhaling the words like they're poison I'm pushing away from me. The look on his face is almost comical at first. He lifts an eyebrow as a smile races across his lips.

"You want out," he says with a chuckle.

"That's right," I tell him. "I'm already carrying one of your clan's children inside of me. I want there to be an end to this. I want to walk away from this."

"Claire," Rufus says, standing up and approaching the bar. I watch him making himself a drink as he talks. The way he does it is so leisurely and so casually that it's almost insulting. "You seem to be having some sort of impairment in understanding the value you possess to us."

"No," I shake my head. "I understand how valuable this is to you, but this pregnancy is accelerated. My body isn't equipped to handle it and the only person who knows how to help me or guide anyone in helping me is locked away or dead. I know that you want the future of your clan and I'm willing to give you that, but I want a limit. I want an agreed upon number of children and your word that you'll honor it when we've reached the limit."

Rufus stares at me for a moment, watching me with his distant eyes as he sips at his drink, savoring it as I sit wallowing under that gaze. "You intrigue me, Claire," he says after a moment. "Before I answer the lunacy of this request, how do you know that I'll keep your agreement?"

"I can't possibly know," I say to him bluntly. "But there are things that I can do to make this unfavorable for you."

He stares at me for a moment, weighing the worth of those words. As I look at him, I know that he's fully aware of what I could mean by that. I could starve myself, poison myself, injure the fetus, or do any number of things that could jeopardize my ability to carry these children. Unless he plans on chaining me to a wall and raping me repeatedly, then he's going to need my cooperation. He knows that I know this and we're at a bit of a standstill.

"The future of my people depends upon you," Rufus says coldly. "We have never had a vessel that has had such a generous and agreeable body. It would be a shame not to utilize the bounty of your body for all it's worth, Claire. I'm willing to negotiate some sort of agreement with you, but here are my terms. First, I want your agreement that you'll keep your physical allure. I'm partial to a pretty face and a matching body. Agreeable?"

"Fine," I tell him. Eating all of this garbage isn't helping me emotionally. I'm eager to get back to eating healthy. Honestly, whether he wanted it or not, I was planning to keep my figure. It's not something that I'm willing to give up. "What else?"

"I want twenty children," he says flatly.

"Twenty?" I say, completely floored by that number. "You expect me to give birth to twenty children?"

"Roman told me how much you love children," Rufus says with a shrug. "After you give birth to his one, then we may begin subtracting from the twenty, but any less than that would be a waste time for both of us. I need an army, Claire, and you're going to give it to me. Agree to twenty and I'll be more than happy to let you walk away. In fact, I'll give you compensation for your time and I'll even make sure that you live comfortably and safely away from the other clans for the rest of your days."

"So now I really am a whore for you," I say coldly.

"Well?" Rufus asks. "What do you say to these terms?"

I shake my head. "Fine," I say to him. "I'll do whatever you want."

"Good," Rufus grins. I can't believe that I'm going to be giving birth twenty one times before all of this is over. I shake my head at all of it. "Now, let's seal the deal," he says with a grin, pulling off his sheet and standing before me naked. I smile at his bluntness.

It would be a lie to say that I'm not extremely turned on by him. It's a definite mixture of the hormones shooting through my body and the fact that I would probably be attracted to him anyway. I reach out and feel his cock. It's halfway to erect already and I can feel the warm remains of Nadine on him.

Gently, I stroke it, helping it along as he leans his head back with a smile on his lips. He likes it. Good. I give him a squeeze, watching the effect on him that it has, squeezing him tighter and stroking him harder. He lets out a moan and I wonder if there's some sort of hiding place around here that Nadine is watching from. I bet she's burning with jealousy right now. That makes this all the sweeter in my opinion. Grinning at him, I decide to do something that I've never quite been fond of.

Leaning forward, I kiss the tip of his cock, gently placing my lips around the tip and giving it a soft, passionate kiss. I feel his whole body shudder with anticipation as I part my lips and softly lick his tip. I've never been a fan of oral sex, but I've done it before. Jake loved it, so I had to get used to it. I take his shaft in and suck, licking and working both my tongue and my lips as he begins to thrust.

I coax his sperm out of him, drawing it up and getting him to the peak before he pulls out and puts a hand on my head. He's breathing heavily and smiling at me and I can't help but feel like I've got him exactly where I want him.

As I throw him down on the bed, straddling him, he never noticed that I slipped the key and necklace off of his neck. It's worth the fuck. It's definitely mixing work with pleasure right now. As I ride him, feeling his warm cock inside of me, I smile to myself. He's played perfectly into my hand.

CHAPTER EIGHT

I look toward the door, wrapped around his cock as he continues to pump me more and more. With each thrust, I let out another cry, another sound of euphoric excitement. There's something incredibly arousing about Rufus and I can't help but want more and more of him. He squeezes my ass and slaps it as I continue to moan, feeling breathless as he keeps drilling deeper and deeper inside of me.

There's something incredible about all of this, but I can't help but want to bolt for the door. He sits up, and I can feel his breath on my back. He wraps his arms around my waist, running his hands over my stomach and up to my breasts, squeezing and kneading them as he continues to fuck me.

"Oh Rufus," I exhale happily, not expecting to feel this great with each move he makes. "Yes, Rufus," I moan, throwing back my head and letting the moans rush up from inside of me, from deep within me. I take a deep breath when I can and let out another moan. I'm more than happy to let him continue fucking me. Loraine and Bartrand were right. I might as well enjoy this.

Before I can climax, there's a loud boom beyond the walls, rippling through the floor and ceiling, echoing through the bed as I open my eyes and realize that something is terribly wrong. Stopping immediately, I feel Rufus's hands on my shoulders. "Calm, my love," he says to me. "It appears that we have guests."

Quickly, I roll off of him, letting him out from under me so that he can escape. As I watch him quickly throw on a pair of pants, he rushes to the window with a sort of kept-together worry that makes me wonder what kind of a man he truly is.

From what Bartrand said, these people can live for centuries. The way he walks, the way he approaches the window, it makes me think that Rufus has seen some things, a lot of things actually. He stares out the window, unimpressed by whatever interruptions have torn us apart. I quickly get off the bed, making sure that the key is safely tucked into the palm of my hand as I dress. I've left the necklace in his sheets, hopefully he'll find it and think that he lost it somewhere in the house. God, I hope he doesn't suspect me. I tremble to think about what he might do to me if he suspected that it was me who took the key.

Pulling on my tank top, I look at Rufus who is smiling with delight. I notice that in the pale moonlight and the warm glow of the fireplace that something terribly wrong has happened. Rufus's shoulders and back are thick with hair, black hair that makes me wonder where it's come from.

Turning and looking at me, I notice that his finely trimmed and meticulously styled beard has changed as well. His eyebrows are thicker and his facial hair is more rabid and feral looking. In fact, his eyes are even yellow, something that I've never seen before. It makes me feel cold inside. He's changing, right before my eyes.

"You're going to need to stay somewhere safe, Claire," he says to me. I notice that he has two fangs sprouting in his mouth and a cold chill runs down my back. "Can you get to your room safely? I need you to stay there until these fools and cowards have been handled."

I nod to him, feeling something sinking deep in my stomach. This isn't supposed to be real. The pregnancy is supposed to be some kind of tapeworm or some kind of sickness, not an actual pregnancy. As I look at him, I'm looking at a man who is genuinely, truly transforming before my eyes. He's in this weird, strange sort of limbo between wolf and human that I don't rightly understand. He makes his way toward the door.

"I must see to the others, Claire," he says to me in a growling voice. "Do as I've told you. Make sure that you're somewhere safe soon. Your room is as safe a place as any. This won't take very long."

I watch him leave the room, the door hanging wide open as he rushes down the hall. I can see the figure of Bartrand standing beyond the doorway, looking at me with his dark gaze. He's as calm as the ocean on a clear day. He hasn't changed at all, but as he looks at me,

I know that he's on to me. He gives me a sort of curt nod that catches me off guard before turning and walking down the hallway, following Rufus like a shadow. That's all he is to Rufus, a dark shadow.

When they've gone, I throw on my bathrobe and look out the window. From where I am, I can see a burning car and hear something that might be gunfire, except that there's no explosions from the rounds firing off. Maybe they're using something else, something less lethal. I don't know how this works. I should have asked someone. I should have found out what a shifter war actually looks like.

"Give us the girl!" someone shouts from below and I realize that they're trying to take the house from multiple directions. A chill races down my back again and I quickly make for the direction of my purpose. I know what I need to do and I have to get to it.

* * *

Everyone is outside and cars are burning in the driveway. One of the windows shatters as a man slams to the marble floor after a curtain of glittering glass chases after him. I've never seen a thing like it. His face is lacerated and torn apart from whatever did this to him. I look at his hands where he's gripping a crossbow and I realize that's what was making those sounds outside. It was the sounds of crossbow darts hitting cars and windows. It seems so archaic to me, but as I stare at the twitching man, I know what I need to do.

The kitchen is empty. I look around at the cupboards as the dancing shadows of fire beyond the wall jump and flicker across the fancy, state-of-the-art kitchen like demons. I don't like this. I don't like this at all, but it's what I need to do. I take a deep breath and head straight for the cupboard where Rufus kept his machete.

Looking at the key in the palm of my hand, I know that there's no going back now. If I do this, then I'm going to be hunted and there will be no stopping them from what they'll do if they catch up with me. This is the dark path that I've decided to follow and that means that I have to stay true and loyal to it. That means that I have to do whatever is truly necessary from this point forward.

That's fine. It's either do what must be done or stick around and be Rufus's baby maker. I'm not willing to sit around and get pumped full of babies over and over again. No. I'll do the deed. I'll take the fall that's necessary.

Taking a deep breath, I slip the key into the hole and quickly twist it in place, feeling it click as the lock opens. The drawer opens freely and as I watch it roll out before me, the light catches the silver blade and I feel enchanted by the look of the weapon. It's remarkable. It's the path to my future.

Reaching into the red velvet-lined lined drawer, I gently take the machete out and look out the window at something that looks like a mixture between a great Rocky Mountain ram and a human. It slams its bloody horns into a man, shattering his face in the blink of an eye and I think that I'm going to throw up at the sight of it. The creature never even sees me as I stand in the kitchen, too eager to continue rampaging and killing Rufus's security force.

From somewhere outside, I hear the long, threatening call of a wolf and my blood runs with ice. That's not a sound that I want to hear. That's not a sound that anyone wants to hear. I take one more look at the machete and know that my time is running out. Rufus is going to make short work of all of these people. This is my time to act. Turning my head, I look at the closed door to the cellar. I have the weapon, now I need someone to wield it.

* * *

"The fuck do you want?" Mason growls through his broken lips and teeth as he sits in the gloomy torchlight, surrounded by bottles and bottles of wine. It's a pristine, clean wine cellar that anyone would be more than happy to tour or even own if they dreamed highly enough.

The only thing that stands out is Mason locked in his chair, wrapped in silver chains in the gloom of it all. Through his swollen eyes, he glares at me, his face a motley pattern of bruises and cuts, all of it swelling together. "Rufus's bitch," he snaps at me.

"Hey," I say to him with a hiss. "We're on the same side here. We both want Rufus dead. So don't blame me for that." I point at his cleanly stitched and dressed wrist where his hand was removed.

Mason furrowed his ruined brows and tilts his head at me before spreading his wretched lips in a grin that chills my blood to the bones. It seeps through me like something vile and unwelcomed.

"You dumb, bitch," Mason says, shaking his head. "It was Roman who got me to talk, not you. You think I'm going to take the word of some human whore? Especially Rufus's bitch? He probably put you up to it. No, it was Roman who promised me a go at you when Rufus was out of the way. He said that I could have a fuck with you and that I could help rebuild the Clan of the Raven. He said he would be fair like that."

I'm not sure what to make of that. There's something odd and sinister in that. It sounds like something crafty that Roman would say, but I don't want to believe it. I don't want to think that Roman actually has a decent bone in his body.

After all, he couldn't possibly be telling me the truth when he said that he'd gotten Mason into the mess that befell the poor doctor. No, now is not the time to think about that. I have a window and a narrow opportunity on my hands and I have to make the most of it. I have to do what is necessary.

I hold up the silver machete. "You know what this is?" I ask him

bluntly.

"The most effective way to kill a shifter," Mason says to me coldly. "Use silver and they're not going to regenerate."

"Then you know that if I cut your throat right now," I point the machete at him just so he knows that I'm not fooling around, "that you wouldn't make it out of that situation."

"Aye." Mason nods to me. "So why do you have it?"

"Because I want you to use it to kill Rufus," I tell him bluntly. "He's in the middle of a fight right now and it's the perfect opportunity for you to hide and kill him when he least expects it."

"I'd never make it out of the house," Mason shook his head.

"Then be smart about it and do it when he goes to sleep after all of this," I tell him. "Do I have to think of everything for you? Do you want me to hold your hand while you do it?"

"Fuck you, whore," Mason snarls. He looks down at his ruined wrist and then back up at me. "What do I get out of this?"

"Revenge," I say bluntly. "What more could you want?"

"No," he shakes his head. "Not good enough."

I feel a sinking sensation in my stomach. I know what it is he wants, but am I willing to give that to him? Am I willing to defile myself beyond what has already happened to me? First Roman and now Mason? Why would I want to just switch out Rufus for Mason? The thought of it makes my blood boil, but in the end, what choice do I have?
It's not like I have to get fucked and give birth to the child right here in the middle of the wine cellar before he goes up and kills Rufus. No, if there's one thing I've learned, a lot can happen between now and the time where a debt is actually due.

"You want a child?" I ask him, cutting him off at the pass before he can even ask for it.

"It's like you read my mind," he says in a mocking tone that I don't much appreciate. I hope they do catch him. I hope they get a hold of him and they gut him before he can ever spill a word about what he's done tonight with me. "Then I'd be more than happy to do this little favor for you," he says to me coldly.

"Oh, and Claire, one more thing. I'm a wily little bastard. It requires a great deal of finesse and skill to escape the wrath of Rufus. So don't think that I won't survive this little event. Because, I will. And I'm going to want my child."

"I understand," I tell him, nodding solemnly.

"Then the key's on the back of the door," he nods.

I turn around and look at the door. Sure enough, it's hanging on a little hook, silver in the dim light of the torch. I take a deep breath as I rush to take it off the hook. As I make my way around Mason, I can feel his eyes on me. He's watching me like a hawk as I kneel down and unlock the ancient, silver lock. It clicks and falls free. Shaking the chains off, Mason stands up and holds out his right hand. Slowly, I hand him the machete and look at the strange expression in his eyes.

"She's down here!" Mason shouts at the top of his lungs, wrapping his fingers around the handle of the machete and taking it for himself. He points the tip of the blade at me and takes a step back, grinning with pure evil on his lips. "The bitch is down here, Rufus! She tried to betray you, again!"

CHAPTER NINE

The truth about everything that's happened thus far is that I'm not sure if I'm even alive anymore. When the nightmares become reality, I'm not sure what reality shifts into. It slips into something deep and surreal, something unholy but clearly present in my life. The feeling is that somewhere out there, in an ocean of oddities and illusions, there's an island of sanity that I'm desperately paddling towards, hoping that one day, I'll find it in the midst of all this madness. But the truth, it's a little more hardening. The truth is that the ocean is real and that I'm the outsider here. Everything that is strange and dark and odd, that's the majority. That's what is real now. I am the outsider.

He points the machete at me and in the gloomy candlelight of the basement, I realize that I have made a grave mistake, the kind of mistake that has cost me everything. I would assume that a man who was beaten and imprisoned and had his hand chopped off would be willing to turn on his oppressor, but I underestimated the terror and the fear that Rufus inspires in men like Dr. Mason.

 The very sound of freedom and revenge means nothing to him. I look into his eyes and I see a man who is devoid of hope in being his own man. No, Mason's hope now is being a savage, a puppet slave for Rufus. He's given up his dignity and integrity for a chance at winning back a little bit of his worthless life. The thought of him on the other end of the machete is horrifying, repulsive and it makes my skin crawl thinking that I'm at the mercy of him. I want to scream, but that will only bring the others down upon us faster.

"Stop," I tell him, looking at his feral, desperate face in the flickering warm glow of the candles down here in the wine cellar. "Mason, think about what you're doing. Think about what you could be doing. We could help each other. We could both be free of this place."

He looks at me with eyes that see nothing, that are completely devoid of any emotional development. Of course, looking at the world through swollen eyes might make it a little hard to see the truth all around.

"Down here," he calls again, grinning at me through his torn and savaged lips. I can't believe that he's doing this. I can't believe that he would ever do this. Rufus cut off his fucking hand. Why would he want to serve that man? Why would he ever do something like this? This is his chance to escape and be free from everything. This is his chance to be a man and take back what is his. I look at him without pity or understanding.

"You're being an idiot," I tell him, feeling my heart pounding faster and faster. My palms are sweating and I'm pretty sure that I'm not going to survive this encounter.

Wait, of course I will. Of course I'm going to survive this. They're not going to harm me. I'm the woman who can get pregnant and to paraphrase the always-romantic Rufus, I'm also pretty fucking hot for a vessel. The thought of being a pretty baby maker doesn't necessarily make me feel too good.

I'm sick of all of them. I just want to be free. "You should be a man for once in your life," I tell him angrily. "You should stick up for yourself, because there's no way that you're ever getting out of here alive. Rufus is going to kill you and no amount of tattle-telling is going to save your miserable ass."

"You think that you're in charge here?" He has a scowl on his face, a look of pure dread and hatred all rolled into a desperate dish that he's trying to swallow.

"You think that you have any control? You're just a fucking slave—a whore that Rufus is using until he's able to find a newer model or you're all used up and can't push out any more of his filthy pups. You'll come and go. I, however, have a long life ahead of me and I'm doing what's right for me, not what's right for us. I don't need you. I'll find my own vessel. I don't need Rufus' sloppy seconds."

I feel rage and fury swarming inside of me and I want to strike out at him. I want to dig my nails into his face and rip it all off.

I don't want anything to do with him anymore. I hope that Rufus does kill him. I hope that the moment Rufus is done torturing me, he'll turn on Mason in a heartbeat and turn his goofy face into pulp. Inside of me, I feel this fire roaring into life. I have never found myself to be a violent or intolerant person, but I am rapidly feeling the old me burning away like paper, revealing something darker and savage lurking beneath my skin. As I stand there, feeling the demon inside of me building his strength, I can't help but think of that old story that people used to tell about the two wolves.

Inside each person is a good wolf and a bad wolf, battling for power. The wolf that wins is the one you feed more. As I stand there with a silver machete pointed at me, I can feel the chain slipping on the ravenous, neglected, forgotten beast lurking inside the depths of my soul.

It's foaming at the mouth, snapping its feral jaws, and clawing desperately to be unleashed. It's the beast that I have never had a problem with locking up. Always be a good girl. Always do what's right.

I'm not blaming the world for being a cruel, heartless place. No, it's these people. It's those who put me here who are the evil people. They are responsible. How can I just stand by and let them continually destroy my life like this, over and over again?
I look at Mason and all I want to do is let the bad girl finally die. I want to let her slip into the dark waters and have her peace.
"You have no idea what I'm capable of," I tell him.

I would like to think that this is just a man thing, that his testosterone-fueled ego is something so ridiculous that it has deteriorated him to an 80's action movie villain, but it's this whole house.

It's this whole world that these shifters live in. Some people who read and saw *Twilight* and *Shifters* must have thought that they were the sexiest and most powerful things on the planet. Well, I don't find them sexy and I don't find them impressive. I find them naively living in a fish bowl of their own existence. These are people who could be helping make the world a better place, but instead, they're satisfied with being horrors and demons to the world. How does that make sense?

I hear the door upstairs in the kitchen opening and footsteps at the top of the sloping tunnel leading down to us. A cold chill runs down my spine. If they believe Mason, then the deal that I've made with Rufus as a distraction will be gone. Everything will be gone. They will probably do exactly what Mason and I think and tie me up down here to get pregnant, give birth, and repeat until I'm dead or can't do it. And, if that's the case, then they'll kill me.

"What's going on down there?" I hear a voice bark. A wave of terror washes over me. It's Bartrand. If there was a person here who could read people easiest, it's Bartrand. No matter what I say to him, he's going to come down here and see that I tried to turn Mason loose on Rufus and he's going to end me. I close my eyes.

Everything was so terrible before. I was a prisoner, impregnated through conspiracy, and made privy to a dark underworld that I never wanted to know existed. The thought of all of this makes me nauseous. It makes me nervous. I just want to scream. I want to throw my hands into the air and give it all up. Just rape me into extinction. Why should I fight anymore?

"I've got her," Mason shouts up. "She tried coercing me into killing Rufus on her behalf." The flickering candlelight catches in his barely open eye that's still good and I see the wicked betrayal lurking there.

I have to survive. I won't let Mason be the end of me. Swallow that sorrow and that fear, I tell myself. Get in there and fight. You're not dying because of stupid Mason's betrayal. I have to go out fighting, but fighting Bartrand is insanity. I open my eyes. What was the point of the Art of War? There are many ways to fight.

"Bartrand, don't listen to him," I say with a quavering voice. "He told me that he would kill me so that Rufus couldn't have me if I didn't help him. He said that he would get out and murder me, unless I set him free. So I did and now he's trying to make it look like he's a hero so he can get closer to Rufus. He wants to kill Rufus, Bartrand. Don't trust a word he says."

Bartrand's dark shadow steps into the dim light of the basement and looks at me. His face is covered with thick hair and his yellow eyes are gleaming with adrenaline that is pounding through his system. He is coated in a thick layer of blood that makes me shiver at the sight of it. His clothing has been torn to shreds, completely ruined by his transformation that is starting to return back to his human form. I look at his eyes, darting from Mason to myself, full of doubt and suspicion. But eventually his eyes settle on the silver machete.

"How did you get that?" Bartrand asks him. Mason looks at him with a scared, skittering demeanor that does him no credit. He's too jumpy.

"I took it from the bitch," he says, jabbing the blade at me. The sight of him inching the blade rapidly toward me sets Bartrand on edge, uneasy at the sight of my life in peril. I feel a flicker of hope inside of me, brief and bright like a spark shooting out of the darkness and vanishing. "She wanted me to chop off Rufus' head or something. I took it from her and made sure that she didn't run away."

Bartrand looks at me, clearly finding the words coming out of Mason's mouth compelling but not in an eclipsing fashion. I'm not out of the fight just yet. "Do what you have to," I tell Bartrand with a shrug. "But don't let him out of your sight or near Rufus, because he wants to kill him. He wants to kill him and take me for himself and I'm not interested in changing one slave master for another. Don't let him near me."

"Give me the blade," Bartrand says to him with a cold, determined voice.

"You've got to be shitting me," Mason growls. I want to smile, but I bite back the feeling and watch as Mason's paranoia and terror turn against him. I don't have to say anything now. So long as there's a speck of doubt in Bartrand's voice, whatever Mason does next will determine if I succeed or not. If he acts hysterically, like I'm witnessing now, then Bartrand will be siding with me.

"The bitch is lying to you," Mason shrieks, turning the blade and pointing it at Bartrand now. Bartrand slowly lifts his hands and takes a step back. "Damn it, I'm doing you a favor here."

"I'm not saying I believe her," Bartrand says to Mason coldly. "All I'm saying is I want you to give me the blade. Nice, and slow."

"Screw you, man," Mason snarls at him angrily. "Where's Rufus? He'll listen to me. The bitch took the key off him. I know he keeps the key to this blade on him at all times. You don't let some whore get a hold of this."

"I know," Bartrand tells him calmly, not trying to escalate the situation any. "But, you're Rufus' prisoner, Mason. Give me the blade and show me that you're telling me the truth."

"Only if you swear you're not going to tie me up again," Mason says desperately. I smile. I can't help but smile. He is sealing his own fate for me and there's nothing that I'm ever going to have to do. All I have to do is stand back. But, just in case, I take a step back from Mason and his jumpy blade.

"I can't make that promise," Bartrand says coldly. "When Rufus gets here, he'll make that call."

"Bullshit," Mason snarls.

I take a step back just in time. Bartrand, all three hundred pounds of sculpted, perfected mass, launches at Mason like he's wound up on a spring. Flying at him with speeds that I can hardly comprehend, Bartrand slams Mason into the wooden foundational pillar that is keeping the building above us from sinking down and turning us into pancakes.

The slam of their weight shatters the support to splinters, fracturing the rest of the wooden pole as it bows and snaps in a fraction of a second. I jump at the sound and sight of it, knowing that at any second, they might bring the weight of their mortal combat toward me.

I take another step back, hiding behind a wall of wine bottles evenly stacked on their racks. I can barely see as something that looks like feathers shoots up in a plume. I feel sick to my stomach, Mason is transforming to God only knows what. I look at the shadowy figures slamming each other into walls, shattering glass bottles, and snarling with noises that are so far from human that it's impossible to tell who is making what noise.

Now would be the time. I know that if I want to be smart, I should use this distraction to my advantage and get out of here, find a way to escape this house and move onto greener pastures as fast as I can. They'll track me. They'll hound me no matter where I go and I'm sure men and women that turn into wolves would be able to track me somehow. The thought of them behind me, following me, is not something I look forward to, but that's going to be my lot in life. I'm going to be stuck with them, no matter where I go in life. They will always be in the shadows, watching me.

There's a loud boom and a shriek. From the sounds of all of the fighting, I have no doubt that Bartrand is winning this one. A beaten and maimed Mason stands no chance to the warmed up, blood thirsty monster that is Bartrand. From the moment I met him, I knew that he was no good, that he was trouble. I knew that there was something beyond those cold, icy eyes that meant trouble and danger. It does not surprise me in the slightest that he's winning this fight. Even with the advantage of the weapon, Mason is still missing his left hand. I doubt he can even see through one of his eyes. He's fighting blinded.

After the shriek, there are a few more sounds -- the scary, quieter sounds of a fight, the sounds that denote the end. The scuffling of feet, the few last desperate twists and attempts to escape, and then, when the silent stillness pervades the gloomy world of the wine cellar, I know that one of them is dead. I don't know who for certain, but I hope that it's Bartrand. That man is an animal, even without the ability to shift into some kind of horrid monster. Hunkered in the darkness, I listen, waiting for the sounds of someone to move, but the silence is all that I hear. It drags on for minutes, building a sort of wormhole that drags out the absence of noise for unbearable lengths. I slowly peek through the wine rack, trying to get a glimpse of what is happening.

Mason is dead. That much is certain. I can see his legs stretched out across the floor of the cellar, unmoving and bloodied. His body is drawn back into the dark shadows of another wine rack, mercifully hiding the extent of the damage that was done to him. He doesn't move and he doesn't make a sound. In the shadows, sitting, is the figure of Bartrand, enormous and hulking, clearly some sort of beast that I don't want to see, that I don't want to know about. He's not like the others. He's something else, some kind of hybrid monster that dwarfs all the others.

I scream at the feeling of a hand on my shoulder. I jump and the wine rack rattles a hundred bottles that are probably older than rock and roll. I turn to look at the person behind me who startled me. It's Lorraine. She's standing in a shredded, white bathrobe that's made out of tainted silk now. She has blood all over her and her transformation shredded her clothes just as they had Bartrand's. I can practically see everything that Lorraine has to offer right before me. I try not to look at her perfect body hidden under the shreds of bloodied, white silk.

"Come along," Lorraine says, resembling nothing that looks like a wolf. She has completely reverted back to being a human. "Rufus has been injured," she says in a stern, grave voice. "He's requesting to see you."

"Mason," I tell her, looking over my shoulder through the gaps in the wine rack. I can't form the words. I don't know what to say right now. I don't know what to tell her. Bartrand has clearly killed him, but what do I tell Lorraine? How did she even get down here? I didn't see or hear her at all. It's like she's a ghost and just passed through the walls.

"I know," she tells me with a calm, disinterested voice. "Bartrand did him a favor. He'll join the rest of his people." Lorraine looks over at Bartrand, sitting with his back against the wall in the shadows. "You heard me?" she calls to him.

"Yes," is all he says in a deep, low voice. "Rufus is injured."

*

Remi and Roman were there when he was injured. Apparently, the sight of it was something to truly behold. Everything that I heard in the whispers of Nadine and Justine suggests that the noble and valiant Rufus in their world finally came to the point where they saw his true colors. To me, he was never a man who could actually be admired or loved by anyone. He was an arrogant man and, sure enough, that's exactly what got the best of him.

In the battle between the united clans that took place outside, Rufus led the sortie out into the yard, joining their bodyguards and those loyal to the Clan of the Wolf. Their deaths meant nothing to him; all that mattered was victory.

Charging into the fray, Rufus took the fight to them and, as I hear it, he nobly took on the bulk of the monsters. Rather than let Bartrand or the others help him, he took on too many people at once. In the ensuing battle, Rufus got himself eviscerated and now, having been carried up to his bed, I can see that his stomach has nearly been torn open from side to side. Laying on the bed, still full of fight and energy, he squirms and writhes in agony, grinding his teeth together as he lays there, looking for something on the ceiling that isn't there.

I look at the bed where, just a little less than an hour ago, he filled me with such euphoric pleasure that I can barely comprehend how amazing it was. Now, the sheets are glossy with wet blood that he only continues to add to as he sits there, gripping his guts in pain, as Remi and Roman desperately try to save him.

"Where the fuck is Mason?" Roman shouts at Lorraine.

"Dead," she says coldly, looking at Rufus with no affection in her eyes. Svetlana and Nadine seem to be the only two who are having an emotional reaction to this. Both of them are torn up, beat, and bloodied, but they are not concerned about their wounds. They don't even hesitate for a moment trying to save Rufus, but I watch the others; they're slower, lazy almost.

Not only is everyone wounded, but they are tired looking. I don't blame them. They just finished fighting for their very lives. Now, they're saving the foolhardy Rufus from his own stupidity.

"Dead?" Nadine turns and looks at Lorraine with looming wrath in her eyes. She's waiting to explode and again, I feel extremely nervous about being in this room right now.

"He tried killing the vessel," Lorraine says, looking at me with something hidden behind those eyes of hers. She doesn't use my name, which alarms me, but I'm praying that it's just for show. She's the Matriarch here. "Bartrand ended his miserable life."

"We need him," Nadine snarls, looking at me with hatred and rage boiling up through her voice. "We need a doctor who knows how to work with our kind. We need someone to save Rufus' life."

"Look at him," Lorraine says, the coldness lingering in her frigid voice. "The fool got his gut ripped open. There's nothing that Mason could do now, even if he wanted to help the man who chopped his hand off."

I can feel Roman's eyes on me and I don't like them. I can't help but think about what Mason said, validating everything that Roman told me in that single, fleeing moment that we were together. I don't like the thought of having Roman as my guardian angel. I do not want him to be on my side, ever.

Taking a moment to realize that everything I did, plotting to turn Mason on Rufus, all of it, was useless. If only I had known earlier that Rufus was going to get himself killed in this fight, I would have left all the subterfuge and all of the cunning behind. I would have abandoned everything. I shake my head at my own foolishness. Fate is cruel.

"Where is Bartrand?" Nadine growls.

"You will do nothing to him," Lorraine says coldly. Nadine's eyes shoot to her defiantly and Lorraine holds her glare. "I am in charge here until the new Patriarch comes. You will do everything that I tell you. Do you understand completely what I have told you?"

Nadine doesn't answer. She reaches down and puts her arm on Rufus' shredded bicep. He's nothing but a corpse, waiting to die, and I don't think that Lorraine is going to save him. I stand there, shaking and trembling with fear as I look at a completely ravaged body. Rufus is also quivering, trembling as he lays there, dying. His eyes shift, turning to look at me as he stands on the threshold of the end.

"My dear, Claire," he says, his voice hissing as he sucks in his breath, fighting off the pain. "My beautiful prize. Those bastards got the better of me." I can see the torment and the agony twisting in his expressions as he battles to keep control over the situation. It would be a mercy for him to just die, to just slip off into oblivion. I watch him, thinking about how much I hate the man before me. The sight of a ruined body is something that I would have a reaction to, no matter who it is. But knowing deep down, beyond the horror, that Rufus is the man dying right here, it makes me still inside. It makes me feel nothing but a numb sense of disdain. *Good riddance* rolls around my head as I look at him. "Save our people," he says weakly, fumbling for the words as he lays there.

How vain and stupid is he? I look at him dying and I say nothing to him, watching him with a cold, expression, devoid of any of the emotion that he is no doubt hoping to instill in me. I watch him with apathy, something that no human being deserves, but Rufus has earned it. He's fought really hard for apathy and as he lies there, sucking in his few, final breaths, I have nothing to say to him that I dare utter while I'm surrounded by these people.

"What happens now?" I ask Lorraine, whispering in her ear as Rufus grimaces in agony, looking at the roof as he growls through his clenched teeth.

"He dies," she answers coldly, turning and looking at me with unforgiving eyes. Her frigid demeanor is something unrelenting and she offers no apologies for. I respect that. The more time I spend here, the more I'm beginning to truly like Lorraine.

"When he's dead, we'll send word to his brother, Robert. When he arrives, the three brothers will all decide who is the next Patriarch. They will also decide if there's to be any bloodshed in the process. After all, no one likes having competition around and no one likes being told that they're number two."

I don't like the sound of that. I don't like the sound of that, especially since I'm here. I'm like a prize for them to fight over and no matter who comes out on top, I'm certain that their first decree as Patriarch will be to take me upstairs to Rufus' room and fuck me into another pregnancy. God, I hate this. I look at Roman who is tending to his brother, stitching up wounds that are going to become infected and kill him, no matter what they do. The amount of damage that has been done to Rufus' body is beyond repair. I'm sure if they dropped him off in an emergency room, all the doctors could do is make him comfortable.

"Who is available for the position of Patriarch?" I ask her, feeling like this is the worst possible time to be bringing up this topic, but she seems distant enough that she doesn't really need to be here in the present. Her mind is elsewhere. Her mind is wandering. But from where I'm standing, if it comes to infighting, my money is on

Bartrand. The man is enormous and if Bartrand is in charge, I think I might be able to work with him. He's reasonable, strangely nice to me, and I think that he does have a crush on me. Power has a way of corrupting and with everything being so extreme with these creatures, I can only imagine what political corruption will take the form as.

"Robert, Roman, and Remi," she tells me in a hushed whisper.

"What about Bartrand?" I ask her, fearing that Roman might be the one who comes out on top. If Roman is the victor, I have no doubt in my mind that he's going to keep me here forever. He's in love with me. He wants to keep me with him. He'll have me be his prized possession until I'm dead. There will be absolutely no hope of escape. I'm going to be his slave for all of time. I tremble at the thought of that.

"Bartrand could never be Patriarch," she tells me, shaking her head. "He's taken a vow to never take that role and even if he wanted to, he'd have to kill Robert and Roman. Remi, I doubt that he'll care about the position. He'll probably give up his role in a heartbeat. All he cares about is Justine. So long as nothing is challenged between the two of them, he's going to be happy where he is. A shame. I think that he'd probably make a good leader if he ever decided to rise to the occasion."

I look at Remi who is quickly sealing up a wound near Rufus' throat and I can't even imagine that he would want the position either. He truly does only have eyes for Justine. So that means it'll all fall down to Roman and Robert. I've never met Robert, but I've heard that he has his own clan faction that is set up in another city. I tremble to think what he's like. I'm not interested in being fought over like a piece of meat, but maybe the two of them will end up killing each other in the fray. That's a cold and dark thought, but I'd be more than willing to let it happen.

"Only time will tell," Lorraine says to me in a hushed tone. "But I think we'd all better prepare for Robert taking the throne."

I don't know what to think of that. I'm not sure if there's something in my future that I should be truly worried about other than surviving. If Robert is a menace, then I'm in more trouble than before. Perhaps this transition will be the time to make my escape, but then again, I'm still stuck with them following me and chasing me forever. I'm sure if I got on a plane and set the horizon as my destination, no clue where I'm going to end up, and finally crash land on a deserted island, I'm sure they'd come calling.

"What's Robert like?" I ask her, worried that I don't actually want to know.

"You'll find out soon enough," Lorraine says in a tone that suggests I'm not going to be happy with whatever I find out about Robert. From everything that I've heard so far, I'm guessing that Rufus and Robert were not friends, but at least they respected each other. After all, Robert runs another wing of their clan somewhere else. So, whoever Robert is, I'm sure he's going to have the authority and leadership that will make him worth fearing. I look at Roman. Good luck, you bastard.

I wonder how long it will be until Robert shows up. Will he come with his own army of human bodyguards like those that died in the slaughter out on the lawn earlier in the night? Will he bring more of these shifter freaks? After a moment of thinking about it, I feel like sticking close to Lorraine. She's right, I'm going to find out soon enough and I'm certain that I don't want to know. I don't want to meet another one of these horrors.

The doors swing wide to Rufus' room and Bartrand makes his entrance, looking at Rufus lying on the bed, clinging to life like a stubborn child not wanting to give up his favorite toy. His cold, blue eyes look from face to face after examining the dying body of Rufus. His eyes settle on Lorraine for a moment until he decides to speak. "Has anyone notified Robert?" he asks.

"Fuck Robert," Rufus snarls, fighting to get the words out angrily.

Bartrand walks up closer to Rufus and looks down on him without sympathy or remorse. In fact, the only thing in Bartrand's eyes is the reality of the situation. He's not a sentimental man, which I think would scare me even more. He's here to tell Rufus the truths that Roman and Remi are shying away from. In fact, everyone is shying away from speaking the truth, except for Lorraine and honestly, her truth is her cold silence. Those are the only sounds that speak to what's really happening here.

"You're dying," Bartrand tells him.

"No." Rufus shakes his head. "I will recover from this."

"No, you won't," Bartrand tells him. "There is no one here who can help you." Bartrand extends a single finger and reaches down, prodding the finger into Rufus' intestines that are visible under the lacerated, peeled back skin and muscle that has been shredded in the fight. Rufus lets out a howling scream in pain, as Bartrand makes his point clear to their Patriarch.

"You're not going to survive this, Rufus."

Nadine charges Bartrand and flies at him in an enraged fury that Bartrand more than expects. He swings his muscle-bound arm and catches her in the chest, flinging her across the room. Svetlana charges him as well and his other hand shoots out, taking her by the throat and throwing her aside like she's a doll. Everyone else stares in silent fear of what he might do next. "Someone," he says in a calm, dark voice, "call Robert."

It's Justine who nods and walks out of the room, her arms wrapped around her chest as she goes, her head hanging low. I watch Remi as she goes, his eyes feeding on her movements with noticeable worry in his eyes. He's in love with her in the way that most people would love to have someone look at them. Deep down inside, I wish that I had something like what Remi and Justine have, just without Justine having to go off and get fucked by whoever the Patriarch is. If I had two wishes, I'd wish that I had never met Roman or any of these people. Then, I think my second wish would be the same for Justine and Remi. Together, outside of this place, they might have had something special.

With Justine going to call the enigmatic Robert, everyone focuses on Rufus who is still writhing in agony. His skin that isn't ribbons or peeled away, is pale. The color in his eyes even seems to have a hollowness to it, a pale vanishing. His breathing is sharp and shallow as Bartrand stands next to him, looking down on him.

"We showed them," Rufus says with a false attempt to cling to victory. "We beat them handily."

"They're still out there," Bartrand tells him, spoiling his parade. "You didn't kill many of them."

"You're a bastard," Rufus growls angrily. "I thought you were on our side, Bartrand."

"I am," he tells Rufus coldly. "But I will not let you die surrounded by comforting lies. Your enemies are legion and you have snatched a minor, Pyrrhic victory in the wake of your own demise. For all the good you could have done, your defeat was your own doing."

"I'll kill you," Rufus snarls weakly.

"No, you will not," Bartrand tells him.

"Fuck you," he growls, tears welling up in his eyes. "You're a careless bastard that I took in. I gave you a home and a purpose." Rufus growls the words through clenched teeth, trying to make them count. "I made the Clan of the Wolf what it is today. Our supremacy is achieved only because I did what no one else would. I am the Patriarch who will go down in history. I am the one who will be in the stories for the young -- Rufus of the Wolf."

"Perhaps," Bartrand shrugs. "But you will die knowing your faults and your victories. It is better to die in truth than anything else."

I listen to his words and watch as the life fades from Rufus' eyes. In the depths of the room's fringes, I can hear Svetlana and Nadine weeping. I can hear their sobs and I feel nothing but disdain for them. As Justine walks back into the room, holding her phone in her hands, looking at Rufus who has stopped blinking, stopped hissing his breaths, and stopped his writhing in agony. We all know the truth. We all look at him and know that Rufus is dead. I take a moment and look at the man who is responsible for bringing me back here and locking me away in my gilded cage. I feel nothing for him.

As I look at the corpse on the bed that they are all mourning, whether vocally or silently, I feel like I've been given a rare and unique opportunity. Pregnant with a monster inside of me and imprisoned, I'm right in the middle of a brewing civil war. I look over at Remi and know that without a doubt, if he becomes the Patriarch, he's my best hope at escaping. He'll be my hope in a future where I'm not imprisoned by psychopaths and monsters. Now that Rufus is gone, I can't help but feel like I have a spark in the darkness, a light that I can move toward.

I watch as Roman and Bartrand grab the bloody sheet piled at the foot of Rufus' bed and slowly pull it up and over the corpse. It's soaked and stained with blood and as he's hidden underneath it. I feel like this chapter of my life is closing. I can see the end. I know that if I'm smart and I keep my head down, I'll be able to get through all of this. All I have to do is survive a little longer. All I have to do is keep playing it smart. No more mistakes. No more misjudgments.

CHAPTER TEN

I don't know how they got away with it. As I stand in my room and look out the window, all I can see is the dead littering the yard, all of them scattered like leaves in autumn across the emerald grass. Their bodies are displayed and hurled in the most random, chaotic way that no matter how hard I try to look for reasoning and purpose in their demise, I can't see it.

Some of them dropped dead when the crossbow bolts hit them, others were eviscerated and hurled away by the shifters in their bloody skirmish across the property. The estate is littered with the fallen and as I look out across them, I can't help but wonder how they got away with it. How do so many people die in so many horrific ways without anyone noticing?

No one has called the police or sent someone searching for their lost. They just left them. There has to be hundreds of people who died in the defense of the estate and those who died trying to take it. Hundreds of people. Hundreds of bodies. Where are all the people who knew them? Did they just find a whole lot of grown, trained orphans to fight for their cause?

That wouldn't surprise me. In fact, that sends a cold chill down my spine. Have they been capturing and recruiting orphans to do their work for them? If they did something like that, then I would expect them to have treated them far worse than me. I try not to think about all the missing persons' cases that are out there. I don't pay attention to that sort of thing. It's sad, heartbreaking. No one wants to think about all the missing children out there. How many were kidnapped by shifters and trained to be their human pawns in these enormous skirmishes over a baby maker? I hope that I'm wrong.

I hope that I'm assuming and that these people are just mercenaries that are taking the cash and walking away when the smoke settles. But even then, I can't imagine a whole bunch of military style mercenaries knowing that monstrous clans employ them without word getting out that there are shifters in the world. Who are these people? Where did they come from? What would make humans ally with these primitive and supremacy-driven creatures? All of this is so strange, so out of control. Where are they all coming from?

"How are you doing?" A voice asks me from the doorway. I turn around, my hands resting on my swelling belly. There's life inside of me and I don't want it there. I don't want to be the parent of some sort of twisted, sick monster. I don't want to give birth to the next generation of monsters that kidnapped and imprisoned me.

When I looked into the future, dreaming and fantasizing about what my first child would be like, I had no idea that it was going to be like this. I would never have dreamt of this. I want out. I want my old life back. So how exactly am I supposed to answer that question? How am I supposed to tell the man responsible for this train wreck of a nightmare that I'm living that I want out by any means necessary?

"As well as can be expected," I tell him coldly. I don't want to talk to Roman. I don't like the thought of Roman these days. Thinking that he might actually be trying to help me is just more than I want to accept right now. For me, I just want to keep him tucked away in that little area of my mind that classifies him as the monster responsible for everything. Accepting him as anything other than that right now just is not going to happen.

"If you need anything, just tell us," he says with a very serious tone. "We want you to be as comfortable as possible. We want you to enjoy your stay here." I feel this is the same speech that an overly kind prison warden says to his newest inmates.

I decide that it's time to cut to the chase. I look at him with disapproving eyes that want more than this charade that he's hiding behind. He's here and I want answers. "What are you going to do about Robert?" I ask him.

"What about him?" Roman asks, shrugging as he leans against the door-frame like some draconian vampire waiting to be invited in. I'm not stupid. I'm not inviting him in. The answer he's given me just plants him deeper and deeper into the territory of him being the biggest idiot I have ever had to deal with.

"He's going to come here and he's going to declare that he's Patriarch," I remind him. "He's going to take the throne and you're going to be his lackey, just like you were Rufus'. Are you going to call him your father too when you go looking for another vessel?"

"He's not going to take the role of Patriarch," Roman says with a certainty in his voice that is almost laughable. "Robert might think that he's the scariest thing to ever walk the planet, but he's no tougher than Rufus was."

"Yeah, and Rufus walked all over you," I tell him. "So what's the plan, Roman? How are you going to get me out of here? How are we going to run off together into the sunset, safely and happily ever after? You have no plan."

"I have a plan," Roman assures me, but I'm not buying into his little delusion. He has nothing. My best bet is with Remi. I should talk to him. I should tell him that he needs to step up, that he'd be a great leader. I would happily work with him. But Roman, he's a moron. No matter how charming and wonderful he was when we first met, his exterior of perfection has melted away, revealing his true nature. I just want to laugh at the sight of him. "I'm going to make sure that Robert isn't a problem."

I turn back to the window, looking out at the lawn, coated with debris, blood, gore, and bodies. Outside, doing all the hard work is Bartrand, reaching down and grabbing the bodies and dragging them off to only God knows where. I'm surprised that he is the only one out there.

Before I can even finish that thought, I see that Svetlana is out there with him, dressed in pure white, with her arms crossed, watching him and pointing at bodies. Bartrand looks at her with a scowl, shakes his head and just moves on, continuing in his task. I smile at the sight of them.

Rubbing my belly, I wish that Roman and the other freaks and psychopaths of this clan were gone. I can list on one hand the members of this clan that I can tolerate. If Remi, Justine, Bartrand, Svetlana, and Lorraine where the only members of the Clan of the Wolf and came to me with the knowledge that I'm the only hope for them to have a future generation of shifters, I would laugh directly into their faces.

But with a little convincing, I would have happily been their surrogate. I would have helped them. But that's not the truth. I watch Bartrand carrying off a corpse and I know that I can't trust any of them. I'm not built for their world. I need to get out of here. But right now, there's nothing that I can do until Robert shows up and sparks the inevitable civil war that's going to destroy this place. I look away from the window and see that Roman is still standing in the doorway like a gargoyle.

"You should help Bartrand with the bodies," I tell him coldly.

* * *

It's days before Robert ever shows up. Locking my door, opening it only for food to be delivered, I lay in my bed watching television, trying to imagine what it's going to be like when Robert finally does get here. I only open the door for food that I order from the staff, and they act like nothing ever happened here. I wonder if they even know about the bodies and the battle, and the whole death of Rufus, but it's hard to tell.

They seem so frightened by everything and completely on edge that I assume they must know what's happened. The only exceptions I ever make for the people at my door are when Justine or Lorraine are standing on the other side with my food. At that point, I'm pretty much forced to open up and let them share the meal with me.

Whatever they want to talk about, I avoid anything that might have to do with Rufus, Robert, or anything that has to play with the politics. As far as I'm concerned, I need to be as far away from all of this as possible. I need to keep them from thinking that I am in any mindset to even care about who comes out on top of this whole thing. We talk about things that I never expected to talk about with them. With Lorraine, we talk about fashion and share our thoughts on different television shows. I tell her about the places I used to go with Chloe and Maria and Desire. She listens with infatuation, marveling at all the places we used to go just to have a good time. With Justine, we end up talking about relationships. I talk to her about Jake and she tells me about how hard it is for Remi and her. The bonding is almost alarming, but I suppose these are the first stages of Stockholm Syndrome setting in on me. I don't fight it. It's a way to pass the time.

I wake up to the sound of knocking on my door and instantly know that it's Bartrand. He's the only person who can successfully translate a professional, I-don't-have-time-for-this message through the tone of his knocking on a door.

Opening my eyes and getting out of bed, I groan and feel the pain growing in my lower back. Getting to the door, I shake my head at the realization that I'm waddling. Everything is happening so fast that the pain is overwhelming. I'm just operating under the assumption that they're drugging me with my food and water. That's the only way I'm still on my feet and not writhing in insufferable pain.

I open the door and glare at him. "What?" I groan.

"Robert's almost here," he says, looking me up and down. I'm not sure if he's checking me out or not, but it makes me uncomfortable. It makes me uncomfortable, not because he clearly has an interest in me, but that he does nothing about it. How can a person find someone interesting and still have no desire or will to do anything about it? I might as well be a ghost to him, just passing through the house that he fancies only once in a while.

"How long?" I ask him.

"Two hours," he says with a shrug. "You take time to get ready," he says with a kind of insight and understanding that is slightly rude to me, but also strangely sweet.

"You want me to get all dolled up for my new master?" I ask him with a glare on my face.

"No.," He shakes his head. "But I know you don't want him looking at you in your pajamas. No one likes meeting new people in pajamas."

I look at him for a moment, thinking about what I want to say and try to sculpt the words perfectly. Letting out a sigh, I give up. "He's going to be the new Patriarch, isn't he?" I ask him.

"Most likely," he says with a nod.

"Does Roman stand a chance?" I ask him.

"He does if he fights for it," Bartrand says.

"I wish you could take the role," I tell him, confessing with exhaustion that I just want to have a face that I respect and that I know would be able to actually help me and not just be interested in using me.

I look at him as I say this, watching him as he locks eyes with me. He only has minor ticks, little traits that give away what he's thinking. I know that he's not as cold and distant as he appears.

"So do I," he confesses to me and I can't help but smile at the sound of that.

It takes less than two hours for me to get ready, but I'm rushing the entire way through it. I can hear others knocking on the door while I'm in the shower and in the bathroom, but I don't answer. I'm not interested in dealing with Roman or shooting the shit with Lorraine. If Robert is coming, then I want to be completely ready for him and I need to figure out what I'm going to say to him. I'm going to have to deal with this head on. I'm going to have to actually get out there and start getting my hands dirty.

When I'm ready, I silently make my way through the mansion, walking down the open, airy corridors, avoiding those going about their business making sure that the house is impeccably clean. I avoid their glances and I avoid talking with anyone.

The one thing that I do notice is that the doors in every hallway are still closed, still locked away from me. As I walk through the hallways, I feel nervous. I feel like I'm trembling with excitement like a little girl. I have to be strong. I have to be tough.

Walking down the stairs, I see that the others are there, standing in the atrium talking to one another. One thing that I notice is that all the women are dressed in hardly anything. They are showing off what they have to offer Robert or Roman, whoever is going to come out of this thing as the new Patriarch. I can't imagine living in a place or a world where I'm just a sexual pleasure for some man in charge to enjoy.

It's like I'm living in some sultan's harem. At the bottom of the stairs, I expect all of them to turn and start talking to me, but instead, their attention is brought to outside where the sounds of blasting, roaring motorcycles draw their attention.

I follow them through the foyer and outside, feeling the cool breeze and the kiss of the warm sunlight as I watch four motorcycles pulling up the driveway and rounding the fountain that was badly damaged in the skirmish that happened weeks ago. They have been slow to repair the feature, but there are others working on it right now. They stop their labor and turn to look at the men on the motorcycles.

The man at the front of the pack is an older man with long, silver hair that is pulled back in a loose ponytail. He's wearing all leather and has a beard that he's braided at the front, like a snake coming down from his chin. He looks around with a hooked nose that looks like it's been broken a few too many times. Next is a bald man with a thick black beard, wearing a leather vest with patches sewn onto it and a pair of torn and frayed jeans. The moment he pulls up, he looks at me and his eyes don't leave me. Without even having to ask the question, I know that this is Robert. This is our new king.

Behind him is a younger man with dark skin and dreadlocks that are bound together in a ponytail as well. He's also wearing a leather vest and leather pants. He is far more interested in everyone around me and couldn't care less about me. The sight of him makes me uneasy because he has the kind of wild, feral energy that would make me avoid him if I ever met him out in the real world.

The last one coming up is a woman who is waspy and has a short pixie cut with her hair dyed blue and black. She has sharp features and looks like she's the mean kind of spirit who would be more than willing to get her knuckles bruised and bloody if someone crosses her. Unlike the women living in Rufus' harem, this woman is not beautiful. In fact, she just looks tough to me. There's nothing soft or appealing about her.

When they shut off their motorcycles, they all dismount and stand around, looking at the exterior of the mansion and all the destruction that has happened in the past battle that overwhelmed the estate. Eventually, they turn their attention back to those of us standing in front of the house, ready to greet them.

Roman, Remi, and Bartrand step forward, looking at Robert with the same kind of determination that they had when they faced down the meeting between the clans earlier. The old man and the dark-skinned man flank Robert, and the woman comes up behind him, looking over his shoulder at the other women that are here.

"It's good to be home," Robert says in a deep, gruff voice that sounds like it's been ravaged for too long by cigarettes. It's worn and battered, like some beat up hotrod that still rumbles on. "I hear my brother died like a warrior."

"More or less," Bartrand answers.

"We're grateful you finally made it here," Roman says, in a voice that suggests that he's anything but happy.

"It's a long way from Albuquerque," Robert says with a tone that picked up the subtlety of Roman's true emotions all too clearly. I hate this. I feel like we're all standing on the precipice of something terrible. Roman looks at the men behind him and Robert picks up on that as well. "These are Hank, Francois, and Carol. They're what's left of the Albuquerque pack."

"What happened?" Remi asks, amused by the sound of that. "Get a little too cocky out in the desert?"

"The Coyotes didn't take too kindly to our arrival," Robert shrugs. "We gave them hell, though. For thousands of years they've sat out there in the Mojave. We weren't going to take them in one fight."

"Tough luck," Remi says, completely unsympathetic.

Robert ignores him and looks directly at me with his cruel, hungry eyes. "So you must be my brother's prized vessel," he says, looking me up and down. "I'd be lying if I said that I'm not tempted to declare myself Patriarch right now, just so I can have you as my own." Robert looks away from me and stares directly into Roman's eyes. "Actually, on second thought, I think that's exactly what I'll do, brother."

CHAPTER ELEVEN

"I don't like them," I tell Lorraine as she lays on my bed with her arms hanging over her head, dangling over the side of the bed, shaking her head. "I'm not letting that man touch me."

"I know," Justine says, curled up against my headboard. "I heard him talking to that one from New Orleans. He said that he's more than willing to share the bounty of his role for his help as enforcement. He's just going to whore us out to his friends." She shoots a glance toward me and grimaces. "Sorry," she says with a shrug. "Sometimes I forget."

"No problem," I tell her with a sigh. I give Lorraine a kick. "What are you going to do? What if that scary witch tries taking your position as Matriarch?"

"I don't know," Lorraine groans. "They just look so dirty. No one wants to have sex with a biker. When Robert left here, he was a proper gentleman. What the hell did the desert do to him?"

"Turned him savage," Justine says. "They look like they have more dust on them than skin. What was he thinking? You don't mess with the Coyotes."

"Who are the Coyotes?" I ask them, furrowing my brow.

"Skin walkers," Lorraine educates me. "They're the old Native Americans who have been around forever. They're practically an Empire in the Southwest and along the West Coast. We're all Old World clans that came over to expand in America, but they've been here forever and, unlike the mortal Native Americans, they're not budging. They've killed more shifters than any other clan and they're all united.

"Coyotes in the Southwest, Buffaloes in the Midwest, Eagles on the Coast, Grizzlies in the Northwest, and Bighorns in the Rockies;

they're all allies and they never war against each other. If you head into South America, there's even more of them. There's no breaking them. All the smaller clans that travel around in their territories are safe as well, but anyone who is Old World is not welcome. They'll kill you the moment they find out about you."

"So how is Robert still alive?" I ask her.

"Probably because he ran away." Lorraine shrugs. She looks up at the ceiling and lets out a sigh of exhaustion, mental and physical. "I'm going to have to sleep with him tonight. Ugh, God, I'm going to have to shower all day tomorrow to get him off of me. All he smells like is dirt, BO, stale beer, and cigarettes. How is he going to be the Patriarch? At least Rufus had some class."
"Maybe Roman will step up," Justine says with a sigh, hugging a pillow to her chest, thinking about having to sleep with Robert as well.

I think about all the times that I'm going to have to sleep with him and get pregnant. I saw the way that he looked at me. He's drawn to me, just like all the other males are. I don't want him or his friends running their fingers over me, feeling me and violating me. At least Rufus did have class. Lorraine is right about that. He had this sort of sage, professor look to him that I had always been attracted to when I was in college. It was like a fantasy being with him.

I've never had a tough guy fantasy. I've never had an interest in getting together with a biker.

"No," I tell her, shaking my head vehemently. "We don't want Roman to be in charge."

"Why not?" Lorraine leans up and looks at me with confusion.

"Because we want Remi to be in charge," I tell them. Justine shakes her head, clearly not comfortable with the thought of Remi sleeping with Lorraine or me as well. "He'd be the best ruler. He'd be the most rational one out of the men here."

"He'll want Justine to be Matriarch," Lorraine protests.

"Doesn't matter," Justine says angrily. "I don't want to be Matriarch."

"Think about it," I tell them. "If Remi is in charge, he'll stay monogamous with Justine and they'll be happy together.

"Lorraine, you couldn't care less about sleeping with the Patriarch, you just want the prestige and political power. You'll have it and Remi will never force you to have sex with him. Bartrand will keep being Bartrand and Roman can settle down wherever he wants."

"But that leaves Nadine," Justine tells me with a cold voice. "She wants you dead and she's gunning for Matriarch. She was trying to get Rufus to declare her as Matriarch for years, but Rufus wouldn't get involved. She'd have to die."

"Or go away," I suggest. "Maybe if they don't want to be a part of this, they could just go, like, into exile or something. We don't have to kill everyone."

"Nope, I'll kill her," Lorraine says with a shrug, completely indifferent toward the notion. "Sorry, Justine."

"I don't care," Justine scoffs. "She's a bitch."

"But there's a problem here," Lorraine says, turning and looking at me. "Where do you fit into all of this?"

"I don't know," I cry in frustration. I cover my face and groan against the frustration of all of it. "I just want to go home and not be someone's baby maker. God, I just want to go on with my life and not be forced to stay in this house all the time." I look at them before flinging myself backwards onto the bed and letting out a loud groan. "I made a deal with Rufus before he died so that I could get out of here without spending my entire life as a baby factory. He said that if I give him twenty children, he'd let me go with compensation for my time. It made me feel like a whore, but at least I would have my freedom."

"Are you kidding me?" Lorraine smiles with a huge grin on her face. "That sneaky little bastard." She looks at Justine and keeps grinning. "When the hell was he going to tell any of us about this?"

"I don't know," I tell them. "But there are better ways to do this right? Like, Remi would totally make a deal with me, right?" I look over at Justine who nods.

"I don't think he'd even have sex with you," Justine says with a shrug. "He'd probably hire someone to get you pregnant with that science stuff, you know? Like the way surrogates do it."

"I'd be totally fine with that," I tell her. I hate that I just said that, but given the options right now, I truly am. I would rather have someone artificially inseminate me than have Robert passing me around to his old man and Cajun.

I don't want to be a part of that anymore. I just want to be out of all the weirdness and the sex. I don't want Robert to be my future. "But I don't want to do this until I'm old and wrinkly or I hit menopause. I want to be able to have my own life."

"Who exactly is going to take care of all these children?" Lorraine asks, lifting an eyebrow. "We're hiring nannies, right?"

"We can't leave that to nannies," Justine declares. "They can't know what they are. It'll be a huge security breach."

"Oh my God," Lorraine screams before flinging herself on the bed next to me. "What are we going to do?"

"I don't know," I groan. "I'll talk to Roman."

"I'll talk to Remi," Justine promises. "I don't know if he'll be open to it, but I'll see what he'll do. I'm sure he'll make a deal with you, Claire. How are we supposed to take care of twenty babies?"

"I'm open for having less," I tell her honestly.

"Much less," Lorraine groans.

* * *

Knocking on his door is probably the hardest thing that I've had to do since I've entered this nightmare. I can't stand the man and yet, here I am, knocking on his door. I know that what I'm doing is messed up, that it's wrong and terrible on so many levels, but I'm doing what's necessary to do to stay alive and get out of this mess. It's time to end this. So here I am, waiting for him to open the damn door and get this done.

When the door opens, Roman looks at me with a surprised look on his face. Standing here with hardly anything on, I feel like a hooker waiting to get paid for a job. In a sense, I'm just here to do a job and get out. He looks at me in the house robe that Lorraine let me borrow and in the lingerie that can barely contain my swelling breasts. I feel completely unattractive, but here I am, standing in his doorway, ready for him to do whatever he needs to do to me to get the courage to go after Robert.

As I look at him, I feel something intense inside of me. It's the desire that he's not as terrible that I think he is. He was my knight in shining armor and now he's just a complication that I'm not sure I understand anymore. I have no idea how to deal with him and yet, here I am.

"Hey," I say to him.

"Hey yourself," he says, trying very hard not to look at my breasts. "What can I do for you?" he asks.

"Take a wild guess," I say to him, feeling his eyes going over me. As I stand there, in the doorway, I'm ready for him to do whatever he wants. I can see it in his eyes. It's eating him up inside, not being able to just grab me and have me for everything that he's craving. "I can be yours, Roman," I tell him. "I can be all yours, but Robert is going to have me if you don't step up. So I'm here to remind you of what you could have. Interested?"

"I'm going to grind Robert into the dust," Roman swears to me, but I don't care anymore what Roman says he will or won't do. In fact, the only thing that I do care about is whether he'll have the courage to at least try it. It's time to start getting rid of some of these problems in my life. He reaches out and takes my hand, leading me into his room. I walk with him, letting him guide me. As he closes the door behind me, he looks at me with those hungry eyes, starving for a taste. I shrug off my robe, watching the hunger ravage him even more relentlessly. "I need you to trust me," Roman says to me. "I'm going to get rid of him. I have a plan."

"Is this going to happen before or after I've been raped by him and his friends?" I ask him.

"Tonight," he swears.

I lean in, my lips dangerously close to his. "Promise?" I ask him in a hushed whisper.

"On my life," he says, going for the kiss.

I feel his warm, soft lips on mine. They're hungry, demanding. He pushes them against my lips, grinding them against me, wrapping his fingers around my arms and pulling me close to him. I feel my stomach brushing against him and suddenly feel incredibly self-conscious about my appearance. I don't want anyone touching me like this right now and before I can say anything, his hands run around my back and pull me closer as his kiss swells and grows more and more passionate, less hasty.

As he kisses me, I feel my heart fluttering. The past claws at me, screaming to come back. I want to believe him. I want to desire him more than anything else, but I can't. I can't let him get to me. I have

160

to remain strong. I have to remain adamant about not liking him. As I let him kiss me, I kiss him back, but it can't mean anything.

He starts walking backwards, drawing me into the room where I was impregnated with this horror, bound to this life. I feel oddly at home in here, like this was the genesis of everything that has become normal in my life that at one point was so strange. It was here that I was brought into the world of Roman and all of his family members.

It was here that everything shattered into a million pieces and I was left to pick up all the tiny remnants. Walking around me, I can feel him standing behind me, running his hands over my sides and my ass boldly. He wants me and he's taking this as permission. I close my eyes and feel his lips on my neck, tickling and sending tingles running through my body. I'm okay with this. He's passionate and he's gentle. That's as much as I can ask for in this house.

Running his hands up over my stomach, I feel him cupping my breasts. They're so sensitive, but I'm okay with it. I don't feel sexy, but it's nice to know that someone out there thinks that I am. It's nice to know that I'm desired. He squeezes me and I lean back into him, reaching behind me and feeling his thighs and reaching around to squeeze his ass. He has a perfect body, just like all the women here.

Everyone in this house seems so ridiculously sculpted that it would make a mansion of supermodels cringe in self-doubt. Keeping my eyes closed, I feel him reach back and unfasten my bra. The pressure and tension of the support gives way and I shrug it off over my arms, letting it fall to the ground as I feel the cool air kissing my breasts. My nipples are perky and alert, begging for him to touch them. I can feel his cock against my ass and it's warm radiance begging to be played with. He reaches up, cupping my breasts again and massaging them, tickling the skin around my nipples, playing with me, teasing me.

He lets go of my right breast and I feel his hand moving slowly, gliding over my stomach as he reaches down to my hip, running his hand over my pussy, floating it there, teasing me. What is he waiting

161

for? I reach behind me and unzip his pants, hunting for his cock. I'm so horny right now that I can hardly contain it and as I blindly unfasten his belt, I can feel his fingers touching my slit.

I keep my eyes closed as his pants fall to the ground and I reach beneath his underwear, going for the hot, iron rod in his pants. I feel it, like a rod pulled from a reactor, I squeeze it and feel him squirm. Rubbing it and stroking it, I encourage it, but it's not like it needs any of it. It's already like steel in my hands, pulled straight from the forge.

I stroke him as he rubs my body, sending chills throughout me. I smile and moan, giving in to the pleasure as he handles me tenderly, knowing that a woman doesn't need it to be rough and harsh to get off.

I stroke him gently, keeping him happy. I want him to take me. I want him to throw me on the bed and have me any way that he wants. Slipping his hands under my panties, he starts to feel me, feel how wet he's gotten me. I gently run my fingers over the tip of his cock, teasing him.

Turning around, I look at him, stroking his cock and opening my eyes, looking deep into his. We might have had something once upon a time. There was a time when he actually had a chance at making me the happiest woman alive. He has a great personality and he has the body of a Greek god, but he ruined all of that with bringing me here, with submerging my life into this hell. The least he can do is give me a fucking that I won't soon forget. I shake off my panties and coax him forward, drawing him in.

Shoving him onto the bed, I look at his cock that sticks up straight in the air like a model of Big Ben. He looks at me with begging eyes, the eyes of a man who is looking for the sweet release that only I can offer him.

I have so much power right now. I feel so incredible standing before him. This could be my life. This could be everything for me. Climbing onto the bed, I stroke his cock and let it stand just an inch away from my pussy, driving him wild. When I lean forward, getting right on top of him, I can see in his eyes the desire that he's holding back to just thrust it straight into me, to have me completely. I look down on him, cruel and unforgiving. He's not in control here, I am.

Sinking down onto his cock is what it must feel like to have a Fourth of July celebration going on inside of my vagina. I throw back my head and let out a moan that comes from deep inside of me. I'm already horny and wetter than I think I've ever been and as I sink deeper and deeper down onto him, I feel like I'm taking advantage of him.

For the first time, I feel like I'm the one being a monster and I don't care. Sliding up and down on his cock, I lean forward and brace myself on his chest, sinking my claws in as it feels like lightning is ripping through me, sending pleasure to every corner of my body.

He clamps his hands down on my thighs as I sway back and forth, riding him with everything I want. I'm taking him for all he's worth. I feel him thrusting and humping, fucking me with everything he's got. He wants me. He wants everything that I'm giving him. I smile in euphoria as he keeps fucking me.

"I'm not going to last," he tells me with a breathless voice. He's right, but not just about this. I feel him ejaculate, bursting inside of me and filling me with his hot, molten seed. I keep grinding against his hips, taking the pleasure that I can. I didn't climax, but that doesn't matter. He got what he wanted.

"You're going to deal with Robert," I tell him sternly, leaning forward and kissing him like he's never been kissed before. When I pull away from him, his eyes are wide with delight and surprise. I look at him, cold and unemotional. I couldn't care less about how it makes him feel. I just want him to know what's at stake with his inaction. "Because if you don't deal with him, you're never going to have me again."

He looks at me with something close to terror in his eyes. "I'll take care of him," he vows to me. "I'm going to make sure that you never have to sleep with him."

I feel the smile creeping across my lips instinctively.

CHAPTER TWELVE

"So you're the prize that my brother fought so hard to keep to himself," Robert says, naked on the bed with Lorraine handcuffed equally naked to the bed frame.

It's hard to think that just a week ago, Rufus was bleeding to death in this room. I don't think that Robert even changed out the bed. There's something about the anarchy and the morbid grotesque nature of it that festers in his heart just the way he likes. He sits naked on the bed, his enormous cock hanging free. Justine is chained naked to the bedpost and sitting on the floor, hanging her head in shame. Svetlana and Nadine are naked and asleep in the room. Svetlana is on the couch and Nadine is in the middle of the bed. This entire room looks like it was a giant orgy, which is pretty much all it has been since Robert arrived here.

His friend Francois is spooning Svetlana, squeezing her breasts as she sleeps, silently kneading them. The old man, Hank is naked in the corner, snorting cocaine while the scary woman, Carol, sits next to Lorraine, running her finger over her breasts, touching her nipples tenderly. No one wants to be in this room that isn't affiliated with Robert. "Strip," he orders me.

"No," I tell him blatantly.

Behind me, I can practically feel the electric tension crackling off of Bartrand who was sent to summon me, just the way that Rufus had used him. For Bartrand, things never change and it's very clear to me that he's not comfortable with it. He's never been comfortable with it, but there's definite defiance in him now. There's repressed hatred and rage toward his new master that I think Bartrand might actually do something, but not yet. Not now.

"Excuse me," Robert says, standing up. His body is covered in tattoos that mean nothing to me. I'm sure he has a whole lot of reasons for getting them, but I've never liked tattoos. I've never found them fun or exciting, just stupid and excessive. I'm perfect the way I am, and don't need a whole bunch of tattoos to express my personality. He takes a step toward me. "What did you say to me?"

"I said no," I tell him blatantly.

"Who the hell do you think you are?" he asks me in a low growl.

"You're not the Patriarch," I tell him, staying strong and refusing to buckle to his intimidation.

"Aren't I?" he asks me with a feral grin.
"You're opposed," I tell him. I look at Justine on the floor, her arms above her head, chained to the wooden, carved bedpost. Clearly, she hadn't been able to convince Remi that he should stand up to Robert. "Roman is standing against you." That's why I went to him days ago and let him fuck me, so that we would have a backup plan. No matter how little I trust Roman, I know that we need him "So I'm not letting anyone touch me until this is resolved."

"Aren't you a stickler for the rules," Robert growls, looming over me like some sort of menacing shadow. I'm afraid that he's going to hurt me, but I know that I'm too valuable. Bartrand will never let that happen. He'll never let any harm come to me. I can feel his presence behind me.

He looks at Bartrand behind me. "Bring me Roman and Remi. I'm curious as to what they're up to, conspiring against me."

"No," Bartrand says bluntly.

"You too?" Robert chuckles in surprised delight. I don't think that there's anything actually amusing to him right now. He's one of those dangerous psychopaths that you can't trust or work with. He doesn't show his hand, but neither does Bartrand. "Francois, Carol, go bring me those two. Tell them we need to have a chat."

I feel something cold lingering in my throat, like a piece of ice that got stuck there by accident and is now threatening to suffocate me. I swallow hard, trying to force the discomfort away, but as the two naked shifters pass me, staring at me like hyenas on the Serengeti, I can't shake it. All I can do is sit there and feel like I'm a piece of meat on display for a growing pack of maniacs. With the death of Rufus, the terrible order that once existed has dwindled into an anarchy that has become increasingly more terrifying to deal with.

If those two freaks bring back Roman and Remi, I'm not sure what Robert will try to do to them. I'm afraid that he's going to try and pull some sort of sick power trip. Is he going to kill them? Maim them? Or is he just going to insult them?

"My brother had expensive tastes," Robert tells me, basking in the glory of Rufus' old room, taking it in as he reaches out for a glass of something dark and hard. He swallows it without flinching. "I once had expensive tastes."

I don't ask. He wants me to ask. Men like Robert like to let their thoughts wander vocally, poisoning the ears and sanity of all around. No one likes a monologue, but some people can't help themselves. It's like a super villain sickness or a Morgan Freeman disease. It is what it is and they just ramble. It's smart to avoid the traps, throw them off by letting them stumble. But like any good addict, those in love with monologuing can't help but pick themselves up and find a way to keep going. It's the one true dedication that they'll always value.

"But he was a foolish man," he continues, taking another sip from his dark elixir. "I was a foolish man, but I saw my folly before it was too late. The whole lot of you, living here in this material paradise, you're bound by the coils of mortals. You think that if you have the right stuff or if you wear the best clothes, that you'll somehow distinguish yourselves as above them.

"But unlike all of you—unlike my brother—I saw the truth. I saw that there is more to us than just the wealth we acquire over the centuries. We are gods. I don't need gold or diamonds or anything else to declare my natural form. I am above all other life here on this miserable planet and I simply exist. No one can take that from me and I don't need to prove it to anyone." His eyes land on me at the end of his little speech. I'm still not impressed.

He looks at me with his dark eyes, studying me, trying to get a rise out of the scared little vessel. I don't think that I've met someone more terrifying than him in the sense that he could kill me with the snap of his fingers, but I truly don't fear him. I look at him and I just see an obstacle, a mountain or a river. There's nothing to him but conquest. He's not going to stand. Unlike the rest of the women in this room, I'm not going to let him fuck me in any way. I've come too far to have fears of men like him plaguing me. I'm above him and his petty existence.

When his gaze shifts from me to Bartrand, I feel something inside of me that's close to worry. It's not for myself, but what he might do to Bartrand. As he looks at him, I can see the same feral, dangerous look in his eyes that I've seen in all the other looks he's given to people. It's like he's sizing up everyone he meets for battle. He's the kind of man who doesn't look like he has friends, but just people who tolerate him and work with him. I don't want to ever be that kind of person.

"You think it's alright to question me?" Robert asks Bartrand, taking another drink and draining the glass in a single, painful gulp that doesn't even bother him. I shudder at the thought of it.

"She's right," he says coldly to him. "You're not the Patriarch."

"Soon," Robert says to him, walking back to the bar and pouring himself another glass of bourbon. I don't think I've ever had anything straight, except for vodka, and definitely not neat. "Soon," he repeats with a smile on his lips that are almost hidden entirely by his long, wiry beard. "Soon, I'm going to be the Patriarch and I'm going to remember this little incident. I'm going to remember how you were a bad little teddy bear when I was decent to you. I'm going to put you on my naughty list."

"I'm not too worried," Bartrand says to him.

The glass shatters in Robert's hand and he shoots a look full of wildfire at Bartrand It swirls and lashes out inside his eyes, fighting to be free. It's the anger that we've all sensed and we've all known was lurking behind those dark eyes since the moment we met him. I don't like the look of this new Robert. It's the true Robert and I'm very worried that Roman is not ready for him.

"You sure as hell better be," he roars violently. Slamming his bloody hand down on the top of the bar, I can see the hair sprouting on the top of his hand, the tips of his fingers splitting where the claws are poking through like ivory heads. He's transforming. I don't want to see this.

"This is the Clan of the Wolf and I'm not sure that a bear is welcome here. In fact, I'm wondering what my brother was thinking, allowing one of your kind into his home. As far as I'm concerned, you're just a spy—an enemy hiding in the ranks. It's a curious fact that my brother dies in a battle against your people, and yet, here you stand, unscathed."

"Rufus told too much in his fighting," Bartrand growls.

Thankfully, the little pissing contest between the two of them is brought to a conclusion when we hear the footsteps of people coming up the hallway behind us. I don't bother looking over my shoulder to see who it is. I know who it is.

We've been expecting them since the moment Carol and Francois left. The cold slap of their feet against the marble and the sturdy soles of the shoes belong to men we don't want to see. I know that everyone in this room is regretting the footsteps drawing closer, regretting the cruel fate that we weren't all born blind. But with open eyes that refuse to shut, refuse to give us refuge, we watch as Remi and Roman follow the naked duo into the room.

"Couldn't put on some clothes before sending your goons?" Roman asks with a smug, unimpressed look on his face.

I hate that he's my white knight. He rode into my life on a white stallion and then he left an impression of the past that will leave me bitter, cynical, and doubtful for the rest of my life. No, that's not even it. Those are like scars on a corpse. No, what Roman did was sabotage any future I could ever possibly have. You don't recover from something like this. You don't adapt and limp on like some wounded warrior, still looking for love.

What you do is burn down the whole thing. You let the flames and the hatred replace the love that once existed. Not the love for Roman but the love that hungered and blossomed and sought out the beautiful things in the world. The love that dreamed of better days like there was such a thing. You burn it, like Cortez' ships. You burn them and move on to find something new, something different. But I'm even robbed of that, because right now, that bastard knight is all that stands between me and a worse fate. He's a ghost of the institution of love that once existed. He's a remnant of brighter days, wholly unwelcomed and necessary.

"My associates have nothing to be afraid of," Robert says, grabbing another glass with his bloody hand slowly returning back to normal, no longer canine or feral. I can see Roman and Remi looking at the bloody mess where the glass of bourbon turned out to be the first victim of Robert's reign.

"Had an accident?" Roman pushes, trying to antagonize the would-be Patriarch.

"Nothing serious," Robert says, dipping his index finger into the glass of bourbon, letting crimson swirls and feathery tongues bleed into the elixir. He takes a drink of the liquor and his blood, savoring it like he's some sort of psychopath, I'm not sure what kind exactly. There has to be a name out there for men like Robert. He savors the drink and sets it back down on the counter of the bar. "I hear you're going to oppose me as Patriarch," Robert says coldly.

"The thought crossed my mind," Roman says. Even now, he's still too much of a coward to step up and declare it like a man. He's trying to play like a subtle mastermind, but he's already two steps behind. I look at the ground, but my growing stomach cuts me off at the pass. God, I hate this.

"You think that's a wise idea, brother?" Robert looks at him with the dangerously volatile look that he'd given Bartrand before snapping and going off on him. Around them, the naked are scattered like bunches of grass tossed into the wind. Remi can't keep his attention on Robert. He keeps glancing over at Justine with a worried look on his face. Even now, he's too distracted by her to do anything either. He's as much of a coward as Roman is.

"I'm not afraid of you," Roman tells him, but clearly he is. Why else wouldn't he make a bold declaration against him? I shudder at the thought of what must be going through Roman's head right now. "When Rufus declared himself, you ran off like a whipped little child, running off to the desert to start your own pack. Now that Rufus is dead, you think you can just come back and run us like some sort of inbred biker gang? It doesn't work like that."

I'm surprised at the balls that Roman has grown, but clearly, he isn't cut out for this. I watch the two of them stand apart, glaring at each other. I swear, they might as well whip out their dicks and have a measure. All I know is that no matter what happens, my life is going to be significantly worse than it was with Rufus. If Robert wins, I'm going to be passed around like a two-cent whore in the Wild West. If Roman wins, I'm going to be his pampered slave for the rest of my life.

I don't like the sound of either of those and they are both worse than anything that happened when Rufus was patriarch. With Rufus, I had a deal. God, why did I mess with Mason? I would gladly take twenty children over Robert or Roman. I suppose that it doesn't matter. I should have thought about that before I meddled.

"We're going to have to settle this the old way," Robert says with a

smile on his lips.

"Why do you even care, Robert?" Roman cuts him off. "You think that the vessel is going to bring us to heel under you? You don't think you're going to be in danger as an outsider for the rest of your days? No one is going to follow you. No one is going to stick by your side, even if you do win the fight against me."

"If?" Robert lifts an eyebrow as he walks over to his dusty, tattered pants and finally puts them on. *I don't care if you're hung, we don't all need to see it.* As he pulls on his pants and grabs his leather jacket, he just smiles and laughs at the thought of him not being able to hold his own in a fight against Roman. "What makes you think you stand a chance?" He starts making his way toward Roman. I feel something sick slithering inside of me. Between the slithering and the icy lump in my throat, I'm afraid that I've got a parasite of some kind inside of me—other than a shifter fetus.

"We all know about how the Coyotes kicked your ass," Roman says defiantly, digging his heels in. "We all know how you came back to—"

The speed with which Robert moves is more terrifying than any viper strike or any bolt of lightning that I've witnessed anywhere. His hand, dangling near his back pocket, flies forward, slamming into Roman's throat and before I know what's happened, a line of blood rolls over Roman's lower lip and races down his chin.

I look at the knife gripped in Robert's hand as he pulls it out, withdrawing it from Roman's throat. As he slips out the silvery blade, I watch as another line of blood rushes out of the wound, slipping under the collar of his deep purple and black shirt. The sight of it chills me.

Roman blinks a couple of times, his mouth gaping and closing a couple of times as his brow furrows, trying to understand what just happened. Robert, grinning like a jackal, steps away and laughs at the sight of the bewildered and dying Roman whose footing gives out and he crashes hard to his knees.

Droplets of blood scatter across the black marble floor of Rufus' old room. My eyes wide in terror, I watch as Roman falls face first onto the floor, Robert wiping the blood of the switchblade off on his pants, Carol, Francois, and Hank all laughing and grinning at the sight of the dying brother.

As for me, I watch my white knight of old, my current lord protector lying face down on the floor, a pool of blood spreading out from under him. I put everything on a man who couldn't do what I expected from him. I had been foolish to think that Roman could do anything. I can feel a tiny version of myself, locked deep inside of me screaming out in pain and agony, watching the perfect man dying in front of me. Everything was falling apart. Everything was ruined.

"Anyone else want to declare themselves my rival?" Robert asks, looking at Remi who is standing silently, looking at his dead brother on the floor of the room. I can practically feel the fear wafting off him like wisps coming from dry ice. No one here wants to say a word. Remi looks up at Robert, his mouth open and his eyes filled with dread and horror. "Well?" Robert pushes, with a very satisfied grin on his face. "Do you little brother?"

THE FINAL CHAPTER

When a person dies, there's a lot of debate about what happens. Is there a soul? Are we more than just electrically charged skeletons covered in meat? Or are we just wasting our time thinking about something that we'll never actually know?

For a long time, I used to wonder what lay beyond the swirling mists of death. I remember when I went to a friend's funeral -- Kathy from my sorority house. She ODed in the middle of the night and when I went to the funeral, I came to the startling conclusion that knowledge is not guaranteed.

Whatever lies beyond the veil of death, I doubt I'll even comprehend it when I get to it. It's an equalizer. It's new, whatever happens. The only thing I know for certain is I'm in no rush to find out what it's all about. I suppose Roman wasn't either. It doesn't matter what we do or don't want. Death comes for us. That's just how it is.

Roman, reduced to flesh, blood, and bone is nothing but a new rug in the room. The feelings inside of me are at civil war, battling for control of my thoughts, but I'm above all of it, watching the swirling maelstrom of thoughts beneath me.

I don't have the luxury of being emotional right now. All I know is that I'm nothing more than a victim in all of this, not a major player, no matter what story I tell myself and try to believe. In the end, I'm a baby-making factory to these things. They're not here for my benefit; I'm here for theirs. I look at the dead body of Roman and I feel like one loose end is tied up right now.

Standing over Roman, Robert looks too pleased with himself, sheathing his switchblade and stuffing it into his back pocket. He never even spilled a drop of his drink. It's sickening to think about him, how easy it was for him to kill. He never even took a moment to hesitate, to think about what he was doing. In the end, it was just bloodshed to him. In the end, it was just business as usual. I don't get it. I don't ever want to be like that. It's like looking into a blurry mirror. After all, wasn't that exactly what I was doing?

Whether or not I'm the assassin holding the smoking gun or the man who gives it to him with a picture, I'm still responsible. I'm still the person who is willing to get their hands bloody for their goals. No, I can't be like that. I have to be above that. But, how? Especially now? How am I supposed to survive this and not be some helpless victim? I watch Robert looking down on Roman's body with contempt before he looks away. It's almost unreal how he just stares at the dead body, almost as if he's admiring it like a trophy.

"Get this piece of shit out of my sight," he says to Carol and

Francois.

We all watch as Carol and Francois step forward, smiling like their leader; jackals, all of them. I look at them, watching them as they grin, stalking toward Roman's body. It's almost as if this is something that's normal for them. The thought of this being normal disturbs me. They're evil. They're monsters. They're abominations that need to be destroyed.

Grabbing Roman's left leg, Francois nods to Carol who reaches down and takes a hold of Roman's right leg and together they start to drag the body off, leaving a bloody smear on the ground as they pull him away. As they pull him closer and closer toward me, I feel repulsed by their actions and as they walk toward me, I feel a cold shiver washing over me.

It's too much to be standing here. I take a step away from them.

"Problem, sweetheart?" Francois says in a mocking tone. His eyes are full of joy at the sight of me in my discomfort. While he looks at me, he grins wider than normal, savoring my distress.

Before he can laugh at me or the sight of my shiver, a hand wraps around his throat. It's not a normal hand, but one completely wrapped in hair and claws. The sight of the fingers on Francois'

175

throat is enough to make me jump in surprise, terrified of the sudden movement.

The sudden movement equally terrifies Francois, his eyes are wide with terror. I turn and look at the man who has grabbed a hold of Francois, but it's no one I recognize. In fact, it's no one that I think anyone would ever be able to recognize. Deep down inside, I pray it's who I think it is.

The man holding Francois' throat looks more like a bear than a man. I have to assume that it's not actually a bear, but Bartrand. The glowing blue eyes, bright as arctic ice, stare at Francois as the former human face snarls in complete disgust. I can see that all over his body, Francois is starting to break out in coarse, thick hair that is sprouting up all along his neck and his arms. His whole body that was once naked is now completely covered.

For a moment, they sort of just stand there, looking at each other as the world around them is frozen in horror and anticipation, waiting for something to happen, waiting for one of them to move.

I look at Bartrand, standing like an eight-foot tall bear, glaring down on Francois with his fangs showing, his blue eyes filled with rage and disgust, hungry for blood and revenge. With a moment of anxiety and horror, I watch as the look on Francois' transforming face turns from defiant bravery to that sudden moment of terror that completely consumes his features. All he does is blink and that's it, that's the end of it. I wonder if he ever had the moment of questioning curiosity inside of his brain before the end. Did he ever wonder what lay beyond? Because with a flash of his wrists, Bartrand lets him find out.

The moment Francois loses his throat, it's the moment that I know all hell has just broken loose inside of this house. It was suddenly very clear to everyone and everything within these walls that Roman would not die without a fight and that Roman would not be the one who left quietly in the night.

Sometimes, even in death, it's worthwhile to have friends. Sometimes even in death, you're not done fighting. I watch as the crimson arch adds Francois' blood to the floor of death that is notoriously drinking in more and more shifter blood.

Francois, his throat a bloody mess of savaged, ruined flesh, pulses with each heartbeat, shooting out more and more blood with each passing second. His face looks completely surprised, gaping in complete, baffled disbelief. His mouth is agape, opening and closing like he's trying to whisper something, asking something wordlessly.

I watch his eyes blink and as his feet give out, I watch him fall backwards onto Roman, staring up at the transformed Bartrand who has absolutely no sympathy in his monstrous face as Francois twitches and blinks a few more times before going still. I watch him die, watch him stop moving and his skin slowly pales as the last of his life is pulled away by some unseen force.

Without a word from her commander, I watch as Carol lets out a shrill war cry that shatters everything inside of me. Whatever hope or bravery that I had from watching Francois die, left the moment she opened her mouth. I step back, hurrying as quickly as my swollen feet will take me. Carol doesn't last as a human much longer; her whole naked body is nearly completely covered in thick brown hair, the color of milk chocolate. As she throws out her arms in her war cry, she charges at Bartrand who is already waiting for her.

Before she gets the chance to reach him, the whole room seems to be exploding into chaos and destruction. Everyone is a wolf human hybrid, except for Bartrand who looks like some sort of looming, enormous bear creature that is more than eager to rip Carol apart. I watch him take a hold of Carol as she lunges at him. He hurls her into the wall and turns. Remi, a dark haired wolf charges Robert, launching toward his brother at top speed. The two of them slam into each other ripping and clawing, tearing at each other without hesitation or mercy. They rip at one another without compassion.

177

Slowly, I make my way backwards toward the bar, trying to put distance between me and them.

Hank, a silver wolf is taking on Svetlana and Nadine without any kind of problem. I watch in horror as the two of them keep fighting, keep ripping each other apart, hurling one another back and forth. Blood flows and chaos reigns. I hunker down, listening as they slam into the walls and the floor. They break the furniture, shattering anything that gets into their way. I wince, grimacing as I pray that there's a way that I can come out of this alive. Right now, I don't think there is. In fact, I'm certain that whoever walks away from this, is not going to care about a vessel, or anything, other than revenge. I listen as one of the wolves howls out, screaming in agony, shrill and long. The sound of it sends a chill down my spine. I can't watch. I can't bear to witness the slaughter of the people I've come to know so well.

Good or bad, I've come to know them all deeply. Bartrand with his deep goodness and hard exterior. The kindness and sweetness of Lorraine and Justine. I think about Justine and Remi in love. I think about how much I admire their romantic affair. In the end, I like the four of them. I like listening to them talk or having them around in the truly dark moments of my captivity.

It's strange that I would come to like those who have imprisoned and tormented me. They ripped me away from my life and here I am, worried about whether they'll survive this or not. It just feels so silly, so pointless. However, here I am, extremely nervous and terrified.

Looking out from behind the bar, glancing at the carnage that is happening all around us, there's something terrifying about the whole scene. There is blood all over the walls and floor. Hair and flesh are thrown around like nothing -- like it's just something you can fling around.

Without a moment of hesitation, I look at Francois, dead next to Roman. He's completely naked and hairless, just like the others. His body looks like it's completely normal, even with his throat ripped out violently. I feel a chill. I'm going to be able to recognize the dead. I'm going to be able to see who is dead among the ruins.

Leaning up against the wall, Carol is ripped in two, completely severed. In fact, there are no bodies left in one piece outside of Francois and Roman who were the lucky ones to die first. At least, there are no intact bodies among the dead. The living stand all around the bodies of the dead, all of them breathing heavily, triumphantly. I look at them, taking a survey of who has survived the carnage.

I see that Bartrand is standing with Robert's head dangling from his hands, held by his beard. Robert is no longer among the living and when he went down, it looks like he took Remi with him. That is, until I see Remi twitch and let out a cry of pain. His chest is badly slashed, but it looks much better than what happened to Rufus. Squirming against her silver chains, Justine tries to comfort her fallen love, calling his name desperately.

Still tied to the headboard, Lorraine looks around at all the carnage without a single expression or thought written on her face. It's almost as if she expected everything that happened here. She looks at the dead and the living with apathy, but I know better. I saw that she transformed when the fighting just started. She wanted to get out of those silver handcuffs. She wanted to join the battle, not look on while her friends and family died. I'm glad she made it. I'm glad that she's not dead. But that's where the happiness ends.

Beautiful, ivory Svetlana is dead, torn to pieces next to Hank who took her down with him. It looks like in the battle, he also managed to take down Nadine. I'm glad I didn't see it. I never really got to know Svetlana, but she seemed nice and I know that she had a crush on Bartrand. As for Nadine, I never liked her. I never even had a moment of kindness and appreciation for her. All I could think of was how much I hated her and that led me down a lot of dark, emotional paths. In the end, I'm no more torn up to see her gone than that I am to see Hank dead.

"Is that it?" I hear Lorraine ask from the bed, struggling against her handcuffs. "Is everyone dead?"

"I think so," Justine says, desperately trying to break free from her chains.

I watch as Bartrand drops Robert's head with a sickening smack that makes me want to throw up. Walking over to Justine, he breaks the lock on the chains that isn't silver and frees Justine to rush over to her beloved. I watch her hurry to him and wrap her arms around him. Remi groans in pain as he wraps his arm around her. It's bloody and savaged as well, but he's still alive and that's all that matters to him. That's all that matters to anyone right now. Everyone that I could possibly hope for being alive is here.

They're alive and that's all I care about. As Bartrand helps Lorraine out of the chains, they all stand around, looking at the carnage for a moment, surveying the death of their friends and loved ones. I watch them taking it all in, the price of their battle, the price of the battle that had to be fought.

There's a brief moment where I expect Rufus to step out of the wardrobe and declare that it was all a part of his plan, but as I look out at them, I slowly begin to realize that it's not going to happen. No one is going to step out and declare that this is a victory. In fact, I look at all of it and know that it's the truth. This is what's happened and I'm stuck with the consequences of it, for now at least.

"Is everyone alright?" I ask with a quivering voice. "What do you

need?"

"Remi isn't looking too hot," Lorraine says as Justine keeps taking care of her man, tending to him gently and lovingly.

"What happens now?" I ask, feeling that sensation of terror that I'm so used to settling in again. Everything feels so wrong. I feel like I'm driving down a highway without any lights on. I feel like I'm completely in the dark. All the markers that I knew to watch out for are now dead. All the things that I should be worried about and watching for, they're gone. I'm left here alone, with the people who are rational and trustworthy. I'm left with the people I actually like and I have no idea what to do.

"We clean up," Bartrand says.

*

"It's been a pleasure," Mr. Josephson says to me with a smile on his lips. I smile back at him.

"It's always a pleasure," I tell him. "The Chateau thanks you for staying with us. If you're ever in the area, we'd love to have you again."

"I'll be back in a heartbeat," he says with a grin on his lips. His wife, Ruth, is waiting for him by the door that Bernie is holding open for him. I watch them go, holding hands as they pass through the doors. I can't help but smile as I watch them. They both say farewell to Bernie who tells them something that makes them laugh, some little joke that he's picked up over his years of working doors. I watch them, hand-in-hand, passing into the morning light and disappearing down the sidewalk toward a taxi that's waiting for them.

"You feeling alright?" Maria asks me.

I don't know how to answer that question. I blink, staring out the window, wondering if love truly is something that's real. I feel like if love is out there, then I should be able to find it. I should be able to hold it close and keep it safe within me, but I'm not sure anymore.

Doubt fills my mind, but in the end, my troubles have very little to do with the actual influence of love. In fact, love did nothing to meddle with me. Love did nothing to break my heart and shatter my consciousness.

Sure, I feel bitter and cynical about the world, but I don't think that Roman was the love of my life. I think that Roman was a fairy tale that I told myself and that I've been feeding off of since I was a little girl. The knight in shining armor just isn't real. I don't think anyone has ever had that. In fact, I think that no one will ever have that.

There are some men that are just too good to be true and that's because they are. They're illusions, most likely projected by myself or others. But there are real men out there and they are infinitely more flawed and beautiful to behold. I let out a long sigh and know that it's not the end.

I won't let it be the end. To let Roman be the end of my life means that I've given up so much and that he was worth all of it. It's best never to let anything be that devastating or that destructive in one's life. No, life and love will always find a way to adapt and to grow in the harshest environments. It never comes the way we expect, but the path it takes is permanent and always there. You can depend on the love that does come. I don't think of love as something permanent anymore. I think of it as something to be experienced. I think of it along the same lines that I think of music. It's there, but I don't keep it.

But, I doubt that Maria is asking me about that. I rub my swollen stomach and push away from the front desk, looking at her. I like to sit at the front desk because I can kick my shoes off and no one knows that I'm barefoot. I like the feeling of being barefoot. It's something that I've come to understand greatly. I'm not interested in having swollen feet forever, but I know that it'll pass. I put my bare soles on the cold metal bar of the chair and smile at Maria, giving her what she wants.

"I'll live," I tell her with a brave tone in my voice.

"I think that you are so brave," she tells me, looking back at her screen to fill out the last of the form she's working on. "I don't think I could ever do what you're doing, no matter how much they're willing to pay for it."

"Being a surrogate is hard," I confess to her, even though she'll never understand the half of what I'm going through. "But they pay very well and a girl's got to pay the bills."

"You do pay the bills," Desire says, coming back from her break. "You pay the bills hella well. But I understand. You got to pay for those vacations somehow and the Chateau is not paying you that well."

"They're not vacations," I say, defending my lie. "I have to make sure that she's well. No one takes care of my grandmother anymore and she needs people to go visit her."

They've all bought into the lie. A grandmother from my distant past has returned and made contact with me. I vanished on a trip to reconnect with her and have grown extremely close to her. Now, in her fragile age, I go down to Phoenix to visit her and make sure that everything is going well for her. I love my fake grandmother and I have to make sure that she's being treated properly.

Of course, they don't ask one bit. Claire used to be a girl that was loveable and dependable. It makes sense that the Claire they once knew would be in this kind of a situation. I'm happy to continue to feed the lie. In the end, I know that they'll never be let in on the truth, but that doesn't bother me. That doesn't bother me one bit. It's better that they never know the truth.

"Whatever they are," Desire says. "You and Chloe are going to be besties now, talking about your saggy breasts and your stretch marks. It'll be great going out with the two of you. You can give us all advice on how to get that baby weight off."

"Leave her alone." Maria grins at the joke. "I think it's a noble thing. I would be heartbroken if I couldn't have a daughter."

"Daughter?" Desire laughs. "You're not having a daughter. You're pretty. You're going to have a boy that makes you all strung out and haggard looking. True story. Every time I see a woman who has her life together and is suddenly pregnant, it's a boy. With a girl, you can recover and look fabulous, but not with a boy. That's a millstone that's going to drag you all the way down."

"You're terrible." Maria laughs, shaking her head.

"Twelve o'clock," Desire says suddenly, "hottie alert."

I look up and watch as Bernie opens the door for Bartrand. He walks over the threshold and nods to Bernie. They're becoming fast friends, or so Bernie would have me believe. As far as Bartrand is concerned, Bernie is an annoying little gnat that won't leave him alone. The truth between the two of them is that Bernie has a bit of hero worship with Bartrand.

He always talks about his glory days of throwing around the pigskin after he sees the brawny and mighty Bartrand. I have to admit that when he walks into a room, he knows how to draw the attention to him. He has a presence that is undeniable. It's a magnetism that draws gazes and when they look at him, they can't help but drink him in. It's like he's an oasis in a wasteland of boring and mundane.

"How are you?" he asks me, looking genuinely excited to see me. Granted, to the naked eye, he doesn't look like he's interested at all, but I've come to read him like a book. I smile at him.

"Yeah," I tell him. Grabbing my coat from the back of the chair, I push myself off the chair and waddle around the counter, hugging Maria and Desire as I pass them. Desire says something in my ear about whether he has a huge cock or not and I just ignore her. She keeps asking and I'm still not telling her. There's no way that I'm sharing that juicy little detail. As I walk toward him, he holds out his arm for me to take. I lock my arm with his, looking up at him and smiling. He smiles back.

As we pass through the door, held open by Bernie, I know that somewhere on the street, a glossy black town car is waiting for us. "How are Justine and Remi?" I ask him when we're free from prying eyes.

"Exhausted," he says to me. "Thankfully, they have Lorraine there to keep them happy." I smile at the thought of that. It's been a while since I've seen the three of them, but I love to keep in touch. To everyone's surprise, four children running around the estate is a little more than anyone could have asked for. In fact, I don't think Rufus or any of the would-be Patriarchs had a clue about what they wanted when they signed up for me.

But Lorraine has turned over a new leaf that no one ever expected to see. Children look good on her and the elegantly chic and model-esque beauty has run off all the nannies and has claimed control of the house. She loves taking care of them and would rather do that than anything else. It's a sight that I'm still very eager to see. "How do you feel?" he asks me as he holds the door open for me.

I look at him with a sly smile on my lips. He grins and shakes his head, climbing in after me. The bargain is set and the world is at a strange sort of peace. Whenever I go on vacation to see my pretend, ailing grandmother, I give birth.

It's every three months that I've gone through this routine and by the end of the month that I'm recovering, I'm artificially inseminated. The process is invasive and weird, but I've gotten used to it. It's sort of become something that I'm just used to now. Of course, I have to admit that I don't have my fun. It's always hard going back to the real world, but at least I don't feel like a slave. At least I have my freedom. At least I'm available to be pursued.

As he kisses, Bartrand lets all the walls fall down. I never thought that I would come to like him the way that I do, but in the end, I see him for who he is. He's the man that was there for me. His soft lips press against mine, claiming me, consuming me with a passion that burns red hot inside of his heart. In the darkness of Rufus' estate and Roman's manipulation, it was Bartrand who was watching after me. It was Bartrand who was making sure that I was safe.

When Robert crossed the line and there was no hope for me, it was Bartrand who stepped up and did what needed to be done. He saved my life. He saved the lives of everyone who is still in the Clan of the Wolf. It was in the ruins of my nightmare that I saw my knight in shining armor, tarnished, bloodied, and soiled, but there he was, sword bloody and still standing, victorious.

I put my hand on his cheek and kiss him again, feeling his soft tongue brushing against mine, tasting of peppermint and something sweet, something sugary.

"I missed you," I say to him, feeling his hand on the outside of my thigh as the driver rolls up the partition to the back.

"I missed you," he answers with a soft smile.

He leans in for another kiss. This was not a part of the arrangement and it didn't have to be. As I kiss him, I'm doing this one for pleasure. Roman's son is blissfully ignorant of his true origin as he plays with his little sisters in the estate. The child inside of me, however, is not a member of the Clan of the Wolf, at least, not in the way the others will be.

The child in me is because I want him or her in me. As Bartrand's hand runs up my side, I don't feel fat. I don't feel swollen and about to burst. In fact, I feel like I'm something elegant and desired. I'm not a slave or a baby factory. When this child is born next week, it'll be because I'm in love. It'll be because I chose to have this baby and that I loved its father enough to want to share a life with him. I let out a moan as he cups my breast and I lean back.

By the time we're home, his shirt is gone and we can barely get to the front door before he has my skirt off. I laugh and try to get away from him, but waddling is only good for a few seconds before he takes me in his arms and swoops me away, lying me down on my back. I look up at him, smiling as he kicks off his pants, looking down at me with lust and love mingling in his eyes. I know that it's not pheromones with him. I know that the man looking down at me is genuinely in love with me. He doesn't have to fake it or doesn't have to be manipulated into it. From the moment he set eyes on me, he knew that he was in love with me.

I sit up and take hold of his cock while he unfastens my bra. I stroke it and smile, grinning at him like a silly little girl. I know that I'm smitten; I know that I'm in love. It's the one reason why Roman doesn't haunt me. Love isn't something that I can hold onto. It isn't something that I can fuck or grow old with. Love is something that will always be there. It'll always be something that I can lay back and sink into. Naked and pregnant before Bartrand, I'm not just a piece of ass or a living poem. To Bartrand, I'm everything and to me, he's my eternal.

Laying back down, I watch as he goes down on his knees and I can't help but giggle. It's my favorite. It's the greatest thing in the world and I'd never been into it before him. He's a master and I'm his happy, loving slave and it's completely by choice. It makes all the difference.

I can feel his hot breath on me and as his tongue works its magic, I moan, crying out and screaming without a care in the world. I know the neighbors must think that I'm a whore, but I like what I like and as he licks me, all I can think about is how badly I want him inside of me. All I can think of is that if I told the truth to Desire, she'd faint.

THE END

If you enjoyed this story please leave your rating on the store :)

*

WAIT....

Get Yourself a FREE Bestselling Paranormal Romance Book!

Join the "**Simply Shifters**" Mailing list today and gain access to an exclusive **FREE** classic Paranormal Shifter Romance book by one of our bestselling authors along with many others more to come. You will also be kept up to date on the best book deals in the future on the hottest new Paranormal Romances. We are the HOME of Paranormal Romance after all!

* Get FREE Shifter Romance Books For Your Kindle & Other Cool giveaways

* Discover Exclusive Deals & Discounts Before Anyone Else!

* Be The FIRST To Know about Hot New Releases From Your Favorite Authors

Click The Link Below To Access Get All This Now!

SimplyShifters.com